"When you agreed to marry me, you were happy."

Hudson continued, "There was nothing, not a hint of anything being wrong. And then, within hours, it had all changed. What happened when you left me, Annie?" he asked softly. "Something did. Something...catastrophic." His eyes were boring into her soul.

This was too close—he was getting too close.

"Annie?" He touched her face tenderly. "After all we meant to each other, you really think I would be content to let you go without any explanation?"

What could she say? She stared at him wide-eyed until she couldn't bear to look at him any longer and dropped her gaze. "You have no choice," she stated as firmly as she could, considering her heart was thundering in her ears....

HELEN BROOKS lives in Northamptonshire, England, and is married with three children. As she is a committed Christian, busy housewife and mother, her spare time is at a premium, but her hobbies include reading and walking her two energetic and very endearing young dogs. Her long-cherished aspiration to write became a reality when she put pen to paper on reaching the age of forty, and sent the result off to Harlequin.

Books by Helen Brooks

HARLEQUIN PRESENTS®
1844—A HEARTLESS MARRIAGE
1914—THE PRICE OF A WIFE
1934—HUSBAND BY CONTRACT (Husbands & Wives #1)
1939—SECOND MARRIAGE (Husbands & Wives #2)
1987—THE MARRIAGE SOLUTION
2004—THE BABY SECRET

Don't miss any of our special offers. Write to us at the following address for information on our newest releases.

Harlequin Reader Service
U.S.: 3010 Walden Ave., P.O. Box 1325, Buffalo, NY 14269
Canadian: P.O. Box 609, Fort Erie, Ont. L2A 5X3

HELEN BROOKS

The Bride's Secret

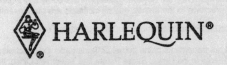

TORONTO • NEW YORK • LONDON
AMSTERDAM • PARIS • SYDNEY • HAMBURG
STOCKHOLM • ATHENS • TOKYO • MILAN • MADRID
PRAGUE • WARSAW • BUDAPEST • AUCKLAND

ISBN 0-373-12047-8

THE BRIDE'S SECRET

First North American Publication 1999.

CHAPTER ONE

'MARIANNE? What's the matter? You look as though you've seen a ghost.'

Marianne heard Keith speak but she could no more have dredged up a reply at that moment than flown to the moon. That big, lean body—the way he was holding his head—there was only one person in the world who stood with such arrogance and disregard for the rest of the human throng. It *had* to be Hudson de Sance.

'Marianne?' Now Keith reached out and turned her face to his, after staring perplexedly in the direction of her fixed gaze for a moment or two. He couldn't see anything unusual in the well-dressed, cosmopolitan collection of businessmen and holiday-makers enjoying an alfresco lunch in the open-air dining room of the hotel where they were staying—it was exactly the sort of clientele he would expect to see in a first-class hotel such as this one in the middle of Tangier. 'What is it?'

'What? Oh, nothing... I'm just daydreaming,' she said quietly.

It didn't work, but Marianne hadn't expected it to. She and Keith had worked together long enough for him to know when she was evading the truth.

'Don't give me that; you resemble someone who's just had a hard punch where it hurts,' Keith said worriedly, his eyes returning to the well-populated tables in front of them. 'Have you seen someone you know? Someone you'd rather not see?'

'Just leave it, Keith, please.' Her gaze had briefly swept the area along with his, and she felt weak with relief to find the spectre from the past had vanished.

It couldn't have been Hudson, she told herself reassuringly. There were probably dozens—hundreds—of tall, dark, brooding men who inclined their heads in that particular way, and she had only seen the back of the man anyway as he had stood looking down over the roaming city spread out beneath them from the hilltop hotel.

Nevertheless, her heart continued to thud as the waiter presented them with lunch menus and took their order for drinks, and her stomach churned relentlessly. Hudson de Sance. He still invaded her dreams and encroached on her days as remorselessly as when she had first left him, despite the fact that she had not seen him in the flesh since that night two years ago. Would she ever get over him? She savaged the thought the second it took form. Of course she would—she *had*. She was autonomous now; she had had to be.

'I thought the shoot went really well—how about you?' Keith was making an effort at conversation and she blessed him for it, although his face revealed she wasn't hiding her shock as well as she would have hoped. 'Of course, the location is second to none.'

'I thought it was good, and you were brilliant as usual.' She smiled, but it wasn't flattery—Keith was one of the best photographers in London and she was lucky to be his assistant. All the top models wanted him, knowing he could make them look good even on their worst days, and he could pick and choose his assignments at leisure. She was a good photographer, but that was all, whereas Keith could make his camera talk for him. 'Those shots you did of Marjorie against the background of the harbour were inspired; I didn't think we'd get anything out of her today.'

'Too much drinking in the hotel bar last night,' Keith agreed softly. 'She phoned that guy she's been seeing earlier and it was all hassle, apparently.' Keith was an easygoing individual—except where his work was concerned, and the beautiful model's dishevelled state that morning had produced a certain amount of artistic despair followed by a rare temper tantrum, only mollified by indulgent obedience of his every suggestion by the lady in question. 'She's a fool to herself,' he continued quietly. 'Why she doesn't dump that no-good boyfriend of hers I'll never know.'

'Love?' Marianne suggested lightly.

'That sort of slavish obsession isn't love,' Keith said flatly. 'Love isn't like that. It's like he's some sort of drug to her.'

The waiter returned at that moment with their drinks and Marianne was glad of it. There had been that look in her boss's eyes again—a mixture of desire and de-voted-puppy-dog appeal—that was appearing more and more often of late, despite her tactful intimations that she wasn't interested.

'Marianne—' Keith's voice was urgent as the waiter left them, but whatever he had been about to say was cut short by a deep, cold voice just behind her.

'Marianne Harding, isn't it? It's been a long, long time.'

She froze—all her senses screaming to a halt—and then forced herself to turn and look up at the man who had moved to the side of their table, his grey eyes of glittering stone hard and uncompromising and his mouth unsmiling.

'Hello, Hudson.' It was all she could manage.

'On holiday?' She remembered this about him—the refusal to waste words on polite chit-chat—but apart from that the man standing in front of her could have been a stranger. Certainly in the past he had never looked at her the way he was looking at her now—his eyes narrowed and as cold as ice and his handsome face devoid of expression.

'No, I'm...I'm working.' Her voice was shaking but there wasn't a thing she could do about it. 'This— This is my boss, Keith Gallaway,' she added quickly as Keith stood up slowly, his hand outstretched but his face straight. 'Keith—Hudson de Sance.'

'I've heard of you; you're one of the best photographers money can buy.' On the face of it the words shouldn't have been insulting, but somehow Hudson made them so.

'Thank you.' Neither man smiled as they shook hands. 'I've heard of you too,' Keith said levelly. 'If ever I need a tough lawyer to get me out of a spot I'll call you.' Again it wasn't complimentary, and Marianne's heart rose up into her mouth.

'You couldn't afford me.' Hudson's voice was pure steel.

'I might surprise you.'

'Very little surprises me, Mr Gallaway.' This time the icy voice was wrapped in silk. 'Isn't that so, Annie?'

Annie. His pet name for her. She stared at him for a moment without speaking, her huge green eyes with their soft flecks of gold dark with bewilderment. She didn't want to feel like this—vulnerable, exposed, frightened. He was out of her life now—he had no hold over her any more. The past was behind her.

'Although this little lady is the exception that proves the rule.' Hudson turned from her pale face to Keith, and now he smiled, but it was shark-like—threatening. 'I'm sure you've found Marianne to be full of surprises?' he asked smoothly.

Keith was out of his depth now and it showed. 'Look, I don't know what you're getting at—'

'No, I'm sure you don't.' Again the hard grey gaze moved back to Marianne, lingering for a moment on the pale gold of her hair—its riot of silky curls restrained into a high ponytail secured with black velvet ribbon—before it moved to capture her gaze. 'But Annie does,' he added mockingly, his voice dry and with a dark undertone that made her flush hotly before she dropped her eyes.

And then he moved on, walking swiftly past them after a terse nod at Keith and through into the hotel's more formal dining room, where Marianne saw a tall, elegant redhead detach herself from a group of people waiting at the plate-glass doors. They exchanged a few brief words before Hudson took her arm, the party continuing out of sight through the doors and into the lush reception area.

For a moment she felt as though she was going to faint, the nausea and darkness sweeping over her in a giant wave before she forced it back by sheer willpower. *Control.* She had to have control.

'What on earth was all that about?' Keith sounded as stunned as she felt, and as her eyes turned to him she saw he was looking at her as though he had never seen her before. 'You've never mentioned you know Hudson de Sance, Marianne. The man's a walking legend in the States—more so since he took on the syndicate and won in that mega trial a couple of years back,' he said bemusedly.

'I used to know him.' Keith was waiting for an answer and she heard her voice replying out of the dark vacuum her mind seemed to have fallen into. 'But it was a long time ago.' Two years, three months and four days, to be precise. She could even tell him the exact hours and minutes if she glanced at her watch.

'I didn't know you'd lived in the States.' Keith sounded hurt, even petulant now. 'I didn't know you'd even visited America.'

'I haven't.' She took a deep breath and prayed for the buzzing in her ears to fade. 'Although he's American his father's family are still mostly in France, and my mother was French. He was visiting his grandparents some years ago when I was visiting relations in France, and we met at a party. That's all.' She tried for a smile but couldn't get her tremulous mouth to obey. 'We dated for a while,' she finished with an effort at casualness.

'You *dated* for a while?' Keith asked shrilly. 'You and de Sance dated?'

If she had said she'd dated Napoleon he couldn't have sounded more amazed. 'Yes, we *dated* for a while, and then it finished. End of story,' she said tightly, meeting his eyes defiantly.

'Marianne...' He paused, and then said, speaking to himself more than her, 'It clearly wasn't Hudson who finished it.'

'What makes you say that?' she asked noncommittally, wanting the conversation to end but not knowing how to bring it to a conclusion.

'His face when he saw you.' Keith looked straight at her now, shaking his head slowly. 'It looked much the same as when *you* saw him earlier. It *was* him you saw, wasn't it?'

'Yes.' Her voice was cool and dismissive, and she shrugged as she said, 'Can we leave it now, Keith? It's...it's history, as they say, and I really don't want to discuss it further.'

'Perhaps Hudson de Sance isn't saying that,' Keith said wryly. 'And I'd say there's plenty that man wants to discuss.'

'I haven't seen him in two years.' Her voice was too sharp and she moderated it as she continued, 'So I would say that speaks for itself. Whatever...whatever we shared is over.'

'Hmm.' The waiter arriving with their first course finished the conversation, but as Marianne forced each mouthful past the tight constriction in her throat the screen of her mind was replaying every frame of the last few minutes with Hudson.

He had looked wonderful. Terrifying but wonderful, she thought, trembling. At six feet four he had always towered over other men, his clothes unable to disguise the muscled strength of his big shoulders and chest, and with his jet-black hair and dark grey eyes his hard-planed, handsome face was devastatingly attractive. But she had never thought of it as cruel and cold—until today. Today it had been harsh and ruthless—menacing—and for the first time she could fully appreciate the fierce, merciless streak which proved so formidable in the courtroom.

He had a reputation for going straight for the jugular when he felt he was right, and he couldn't be bought—two qualities which caused even the nastiest of criminals to tremble when they heard he was after their blood. But with her he had been tender, gentle and wonderfully sexy...

'Marianne?' She came out of the raw, pain-filled reverie to the realisation that Keith had been speaking and she hadn't heard a word he'd said. 'Where on earth are you?' he asked, his voice testy.

'Oh, sorry,' she said quickly, hoping he would be mollified.

'No, *I* am sorry,' he said tightly, his brown eyes narrowed. 'You aren't over him, are you? A blind man could see that.'

It wasn't really a question, but she responded as though it had been. 'Over him? Hudson de Sance? Don't be so silly; I told you, I haven't seen him in two years. Anyway, there's nothing to be over—' She stopped abruptly. She was protesting too much and they both knew it. She stared at Keith, her face flushing.

'I'm not going to pry, Marianne.' The waiter reappeared with their seafood platters, and Keith waited until they were alone again before he repeated, 'I'm not going to pry, but I just want to say one thing. You are good at your job—very good—and I'd be upset if you allowed anything, or anyone, to interfere with that. You could go right to the top, you understand me?'

She nodded mutely, swallowing hard against the lump in her throat which was the result of the shock of seeing Hudson again.

'I'm only saying this because I care about you,' he added quietly, 'and because we work well together—very well.'

'Thank you.' She took a deep breath and managed a wobbly smile. 'I do love my job, Keith, you know that.

It's given me more opportunities to travel than I'd ever dreamed possible.'

'And of course the added bonus of working with a handsome and dynamic young boss who has the world at his fingertips—don't forget that.' It was said jokingly in an effort to defuse the almost painful tension. 'Now eat up; we've got a busy afternoon ahead of us, and all our skills are going to be required to make Marjorie and June perform on that fishing boat. They both get seasick,' he added wryly.

The afternoon went well, as Marianne had known it would. The sun was blazing down out of a crystal sky, the dancing waves were lit with sunshine and the gaily painted fishing boat was a perfect backdrop for the tall, graceful models in their wildly expensive leisure wear. A photographer's dream. And normally Marianne would have enjoyed the hectic pace, the laughter, the razzmatazz that went hand in hand with such a showy display. But not today.

Today she caught herself glancing back at the harbour all the time they worked, her eyes searching the quay for a tall, dark figure, even as her mind berated the stupidity of it. She had seen the stunning redhead, hadn't she? Why on earth did she think Hudson would be remotely interested in following up on their lunchtime encounter? She was nothing to him now. Her life had moved on—and his had always moved at a rate which had left her breathless.

Was his presence in Tangier down to business or pleasure? she asked herself as she stepped off the boat in the heat of late afternoon. And was that woman his girlfriend, his mistress—perhaps even his wife? The thought hit her in the solar plexus and she paused on the quay as Keith and the others stood admiring a huge ocean liner coming in to dock. He could be married or engaged. He was thirty-seven years old now—twelve years older than her—and had to be the catch of the century in the circles he moved in.

'Taxi or gig?' Keith asked as he joined her, indicating the row of light, two-wheeled, horse-drawn carriages lined up and waiting for customers.

'I don't mind; what are the others doing?' she asked quietly, her thoughts still a million miles away. 'There was talk of a market?'

'Marjorie and June are going shopping with Guy, but beyond that I don't know. We could perhaps—' He stopped abruptly, looking at something over Marianne's left shoulder, his face slowly darkening in uncharacteristic anger. 'What the hell is he doing here?' he asked grimly. 'The cheek of the man.'

She knew, even before she turned to follow the direction of his gaze, who it was. Only Hudson de Sance could put that look on someone's face. It was an ability of his she had noticed before.

Hudson was at their side within seconds, his loose-limbed, easy walk covering the space before she had time to think or feel. 'Hello again.' He spoke to them both, his iron-hard gaze sweeping across their faces with such condemning coldness that Marianne found herself blushing as though she had been caught doing something immoral, rather than standing on a busy quayside in the bright Moroccan sunshine of a May evening. 'Finished for the day?' he asked coolly, with a flick of his head at the others who were departing in various directions, before his eyes fastened on Marianne's hot face.

'Yes.' Her tone of voice was as cryptic as his had been, but more to disguise the effect his sudden appearance had had on her equilibrium than anything else. He had changed from the smart business suit he'd been wearing that lunchtime, and now the big, powerful frame was clothed in an open-necked pale blue shirt that showed a tantalising glimpse of tightly curled dark body hair, and well-worn black jeans, tight across the hips. His flagrant masculinity was even more intimidating than she remembered, and it stopped her breath.

'Then I would like to speak with you.' It was as formal, and as constrained, as if he'd been in court. 'Privately,' he added, with a cold glance at Keith, who was bristling like a giant porcupine. 'I'm sure Mr Gallaway can spare you for a while.'

'I really don't think we've anything to say to each other.' How she managed it she didn't know, but her voice sounded quite calm, composed even, which was at odds with her galloping heartbeat and churning stomach.

'I disagree,' he said with a smooth self-assurance that grated like metal on fine porcelain. 'So, if you don't mind…?'

'Now look, de Sance, if Marianne doesn't want to speak to you…' Keith's voice died away as the full force of a pair of menacingly ruthless grey eyes homed in on his before narrowing to laser-like slits. Hudson could express more with one glance than any man she knew.

'This is nothing to do with you,' Hudson said softly. 'So let's keep it that way, okay?' It was more intimidating than any brazen threat, and Marianne saw Keith gulp slightly before his eyes wavered and fell, and she felt a dart of anger break through the fright.

'Well?' Hudson turned to Marianne again, his voice icy. 'We are staying at the same hotel, so I can give you a lift back there and we can talk on the way. Is that civilised enough for you?'

'I've said no, and please don't threaten my friends—'

'Marianne is with me.'

Keith spoke at the same time as Marianne, but this time Hudson's glare was accompanied by a quick turning movement of his body that had Marianne clutching his arm before she realised what she was doing. 'Don't! Leave him alone,' she said breathlessly as Keith stumbled backwards so quickly, he almost fell. 'Don't bully him.'

Hudson was very still for a long moment as he looked down at her small hand on his arm, and then he raised his eyes to her face and stared at her for several heart-stopping seconds before saying, 'There's the easy way, and then there's the hard way, Annie. Which is it to be?'

'I'll ride back to the hotel with you,' she said weakly, her heart thudding anew at the relentless hardness on his face. He frightened her, this new Hudson de Sance. In fact he scared her to death. There was nothing left of the man she had known.

'Good.' Just one word, but it was chilling, and increased her nervous tension.

'I'll see you later, Keith. Don't...don't worry,' she added quickly, seeing the agonised indecision in his worried little face. He was only a few years younger than Hudson in actual fact, but his slight stature, coupled with naturally boyish good looks, made it difficult to believe he was a day over twenty-one—something he capitalised on in his day-to-day work.

The models found him comfortingly non-threatening, especially when he turned on the little-boy charm, and this attribute, added to the brilliance of his work, had made him the toast of his profession, and enabled him to achieve the sort of results others only dreamed of. She didn't have a chance to say any more; Hudson had taken her by the elbow, his grip bruising, and she found herself being whisked along the quayside at a speed that left her breathless.

'Here.' He stopped beside an elegant sports car that was all sleek lines and gleaming red metal and opened the passenger door for her, watching her with a cool, all-encompassing gaze as she slid carefully inside the beautiful vehicle without saying a word.

He joined her immediately and at once her senses registered the elusive smell of the aftershave he had specially made for him, its perfume evoking memories she could well have done without in the circumstances, and doing nothing to alleviate her panic.

'How long are you staying in Tangier?' he asked quietly, his voice seeming to be without real interest.

'Just a few days more.' It wasn't quite true, but she

had no intention of revealing that she had arranged to combine the business trip with a holiday, and that she was staying on when the rest of the troupe left. She planned to join a tour which took in the five major cities of Morocco on the day Keith and the others flew home. 'It's...it's quite a coincidence meeting you like this, after all this time...' She came to a stumbling halt as her voice failed her.

'Isn't it?' he agreed flatly, before pulling off in a great growl of powerfully honed engine.

It was only a few minutes later that Marianne realised they weren't travelling on the road which led up into the hills to their hotel. She would have noticed it even sooner but for the fact her senses were battling with the close proximity of the big masculine body at the side of her.

She hadn't dared look at him, but now, as they travelled along a broad avenue lined with modern stores and houses, her eyes flashed to his grim profile. 'This isn't the way back to the hotel,' she challenged hotly. 'It isn't, is it?'

'No?' His voice was too innocent to be taken seriously.

'You know it isn't. Where...where are we going?' she asked nervously, real fear in her voice as she realised her vulnerability.

'Relax, Annie.' The stone-grey eyes flashed over her face for one piercing moment as he caught the panic she couldn't hide. 'I'm not into abduction, or rape, or any one of a number of variations on those themes. I see the misery caused by those sorts of abuses of strength too often in my work to indulge personally,' he said drily. 'You're quite safe.'

Safe? With Hudson de Sance? Never, she thought wildly.

'You said we were going back to the hotel,' she accused, once she could trust her voice not to shake. He would just love to think she was quivering in her shoes! 'Didn't you?'

'And so we are.' He paused for a moment, and then added, 'Eventually,' his voice full of dark mockery.

'Eventually?' She glared at him, her eyes flashing.

'It means finally, in the end, ultimately,' he said helpfully.

'*I know what the word means.*'

Her voice was too shrill, and she was furiously angry with herself for not matching his cool control, especially when the grey eyes moved over her face in another lightning glance and the black eyebrows lifted in indulgent disapproval. 'Don't screech, Annie; it's most unbecoming,' he drawled easily.

She mentally counted to ten—slowly—and then said, in as even a tone as she could manage, 'I just want to know where we are going. I think that is reasonable enough—to any normal person.'

'Reasonable doesn't enter into it.' Now his voice was clipped, and for the first time she saw his knuckles were white as he gripped the steering wheel. His control wasn't as real as he'd like her to believe, she thought nervously as fear engulfed her again. 'You, of all people, should know that.'

'Hudson—'

'You walked out on me two years ago without so much as a by-your-leave,' he bit out tightly. 'You call that reasonable?'

'I left a letter to explain why,' she protested quickly.

'The original "dear John". Yes, I read it,' he said icily. 'And yet the evening before that you had agreed to become my wife.'

'I explained—' She stopped abruptly as they turned a corner and almost collided with an aged donkey bearing bales of merchandise on its back, his owner having stopped to carry on a conversation with a vendor selling pomegranates from an old pushcart at the side of the road. It was charming and picturesque, but quite how the accident claim form would have read was another matter.

Hudson swore angrily under his breath, sounded his horn and continued down the dusty road leading away from the modern European section of the city they had been in earlier.

'I explained about that,' Marianne said weakly after a moment or two. 'Our lifestyles were too different—I had only recently finished university and I'd never even been to the States. Everything had happened too quickly. We…we didn't really know each other.'

'Rubbish,' he said with ruthless honesty. 'That's rubbish and you know it. If it had just been that, you wouldn't have dropped off the face of the earth. I came looking for you, but of course you know that. Your aunt and uncle were very shocked by it all, but your stepfather not so much. It was he who told me the truth.'

'The truth?' She was losing it, she thought frantically as her mind raced and spun. He had seen Michael? That had been the one thing she'd been trying to prevent by leaving France in the middle of the night without a word to anyone. What had Michael told him? She wouldn't put anything past her stepfather.

'What was his name, Annie, this guy from university?' Hudson asked coldly. 'And why the hell didn't you tell me about him yourself instead of getting your stepfather to do your dirty work and tell me you were engaged? You didn't go back to Scotland, did you? The pair of you simply vanished off the face of the earth.'

'I…I went to London,' she admitted through stiff lips.

'And Harding? Is that your married name?' he bit out tightly.

'No, I…I didn't get married,' she said flatly. 'I changed my name from McBride, that's all. Harding…Harding was more suitable in London.'

'You didn't get married?' She felt the penetrating gaze sweep her face again but forced herself to stare straight ahead, her eyes seeing the hot street outside the car, with its veiled women, energetic little children and robed men, as though she were in a dream. 'But I thought—' He paused. 'Was that anything to do with the car crash?' he asked softly. 'Or a separate decision?'

'You know about the crash?' She did turn to look at him then, but the dark, tanned profile was giving nothing away. 'How?' Scotland was a long way from America.

'Let's just say I kept tabs for a while,' he said smoothly. 'You didn't go to the funeral of your mother and stepfather. Why?'

'Reasons.' This was becoming too hot to handle. 'Look, Hudson, the past is the past—can't we just leave it at that? And where *are* we going anyway?' she asked nervously as they joined a road that began to curve upwards. 'I need to get back—'

'A friend of mine has invited me to stop by this evening.' He had known how she would react, and his voice was dry and cool as he said, 'Don't look so surprised, Annie. I do have friends, you know. Or is that too difficult for you to believe?'

'I'm sure you do,' she said tightly. 'But won't they be surprised to see you turn up at the door with a strange woman?'

'The "strange woman" is your terminology, not mine,' he mocked softly. 'I would have said unusual, extraordinary perhaps, but strange is going a little too far.'

'You know what I meant.' She'd hit him in a minute—she would!

'So...' The cool voice was thoughtful. 'Where did you go when you ran away from me, if not to marry your lover?'

'I've told you—London,' she said shortly.

'And you changed your name and cut off all contact with your family, even to the extent of not attending your parents' funeral.' He was talking as though to himself. 'What made you contact your aunt in France after two years?' he asked suddenly, his voice sharpening into cold steel.

'How did you know——?' She stopped abruptly, her face going white as reality dawned. 'You *knew* I would be here, didn't you?' she said dazedly. 'This is not a coincidence.' He had known her name earlier at lunch. He had called her Marianne *Harding.*

'You haven't answered my question.' The cool mockery was back.

'You haven't answered mine either,' she shot back quickly, his cold, faintly drawling voice incredibly irritating when she was as tense as a tightly coiled spring. 'You knew I'd be here, in this hotel in Tangier, didn't you? You planned all this.'

'You really think I would chase across half the world because I'd discovered your whereabouts?' he asked contemptuously, and at the same moment, with a flash of mortifying and hot humiliation, she remembered the stunning redhead. He was here with *her.* Of course.

'I...I didn't mean that.' She didn't really know *what* she had meant, she admitted to herself painfully. But that wasn't surprising—Hudson had always had the power to send her senses into overdrive and her mind spinning. She hadn't looked at another man—hadn't had the slightest interest in one—since she had left France two years ago. Left *him* two years ago. How he'd laugh at that.

'Here we are.' As the car passed through a great archway covered in traceries so delicate and intricate that they looked like lace, Marianne saw they were in the courtyard of what was obviously a very wealthy family, the low, sprawling white house in front of them decorated in the Moorish style with fine carvings in stone and wood. The air was heavy with the perfume of banana trees, bougainvillea vines and other flowering tropical plants. Several sparkling fountains murmured in the vegetation beyond the courtyard. It was tranquil, serene and very beautiful.

'My friend's name is Idris,' Hudson said quietly as he brought the car to a quiet standstill in the warm, scented air, the sound of droning insects in the vegetation meeting their ears. 'He and his family are very westernised, but he is a Berber through and through and proud of it. We will be expected to eat with them.'

'But...' It was as though she had been transported into another world, swept along in the dark aura of this man who had dominated her life since the first moment she had laid eyes on him—the intervening years since she'd last seen him accentuating, rather than diminishing, his fierce appeal. 'I can't... They don't know me. Hudson, you must see I can't stay; it's presumptuous—'

'They expected me to bring a friend.' The glittering grey gaze fastened on her alarmed green eyes with their deep gold flecks, and then he uncoiled himself from the car, walking with cat-like litheness round to the passenger door.

A friend? The redhead, no doubt, Marianne thought silently as a rapier-sharp stab of jealousy replaced the desperate panic. Why hadn't *she* come? Was she ill? Indisposed in some way? But that still didn't explain why he had appeared on the quayside like that.

'Come along.' His deep, smoky voice interrupted her frantic thoughts, and as she slid out of the car his hand on her arm seemed to burn like fire. She didn't want to obey, but there was nothing else she could do, after all.

This was crazy, surreal—it couldn't be happening, Marianne told herself as she stood dazedly in the shaded warm air. She should be back at the hotel, getting ready for dinner in an environment that was familiar and safe and controlled. How had she got here anyway? She had only agreed to have a lift with him.

'Hudson...please—'

'"Hudson...please".' He mimicked her voice softly and cruelly, his face mocking and his eyes narrowed. 'You used to say that in the old days—"Hudson, oh, Hudson, please...please"—remember? When you were in my arms, when I was kissing you—holding you. Did your young English lover take you into the world we inhabited, Annie? Did he make you feel like I made you feel? *Did he?*'

'You're hurting me.' His hand on her arm was vice-like.

'Am I?' He released her immediately. 'I want to hurt you, my inconsistent little siren,' he said with such matter-of-fact coolness that it took a moment for his words to sink in. 'I want to see you suffer, like I suffered two years ago. Not in any physical sense—that would be too easy, too simple. But I would like to get inside your head—like you got inside mine—and watch while I slowly drain the very essence of you into my control. Does that shock you?' he added with a marked lack of expression.

She stared at him, quite unable to speak, her mind frozen.

'But we are civilised people, are we not?' He smiled, but it was a mere twisting of the firm, sensual mouth, and chilled her still further. 'And civilised people play games, have fun, flit from one partner to another if they get bored—'

'I'm not like that.' Her words were a trembling whisper, but he heard them. 'I've never played those sorts of games in my life.'

'No?' The grey eyes flickered briefly. 'Forgive me, but I'm not convinced. My mother's father, a tough old Texan with a hide as thick as a rhinoceros—from whom I got my Christian name, incidentally—always used to say that actions speak louder than words. It used to irritate me as a boy as he invariably hammered it home when I was guilty of some fall from grace. But he was dead right, Annie. And your actions to date are somewhat—forgive me—frivolous, to put it mildly,' he added with deadly sarcasm.

'Hudson—'

'Or do you consider a breach of faith between lovers

as par for the course?' he asked with lethal softness.
'Part of the fun?'

'No, of course I don't. I didn't... It wasn't like that.'
She didn't want to cry—she *couldn't* cry—it would be
the final humiliation, she told herself desperately as tears
burnt fiercely at the back of her eyes, and she lowered
her gaze quickly in case he saw the betraying sheen that
was splintering the sunlight into a thousand glittering
fragments. But not quickly enough.

'And that old feminine ploy of tears won't work either,' he drawled nastily. 'I'm too long in the tooth for
that. For someone to behave like you did takes something the average person hasn't got, so don't try the
weak, trembling female approach now. There's steel under that beautiful exterior—I know; I've felt it.'

'You know nothing about me,' she said shakily, keeping her face turned from him and her eyes downcast.

'Oh, I'd agree with that, sweetheart.' He laughed bitterly. 'Now that *is* the truth.'

'Then why not just leave me alone?' she muttered
painfully. 'I didn't ask to come here with you; I don't
want to be here with you. It was you who instigated
this.'

'I've no doubt at all you would rather be back at the
hotel enjoying a cocktail or two before dinner with the
reputable Keith,' Hudson said sardonically. 'But unfortunately here you are and here you will remain until *I*
choose to take you back.'

'And this satisfies some twisted idea of revenge? Is
that it?' She raised her head now, her face fiery. 'What
sort of person are you, Hudson?'

'I rather think that should be my line in the circumstances,' he said with a silky coldness that told her her
shot had hit home. 'But if you'd like me to show you
what sort of man I am, Annie...'

He had taken her in his arms before she had any clear
idea of his intentions, his embrace crushing her into him
as his mouth took hers in a kiss that was meant to punish

and subdue. For a moment the shock of being held by him was overwhelming, the touch and taste of him achingly familiar, and then, as the tempo changed and he began to cover her face in burningly hot kisses that made her limp and fluid beneath his mouth, she strained into him, hardly aware of what she was doing.

How long the embrace continued she didn't know; the magic of his kisses, the sheer sensation that was flowing like fire between them, wiped all coherent thought clean away. She could hear herself moaning his name, and she thought she heard him groan against her throat but then, in the next moment, he had thrust her away from him so violently, she almost fell.

'How can you do that—kiss me back like that—when it doesn't mean a thing?' he snarled bitterly, his eyes blazing. 'Who, *what* are you, Marianne McBride—or Harding—or whatever it is you call yourself?'

CHAPTER TWO

MARIANNE had never been more relieved in the whole of her life than she was when a childish whoop of glee sounded from the house behind them, and a small body hurtled over to wind itself round Hudson's legs, drawing away his attention and breaking his furious gaze.

'Abdul, my little friend...' Hudson immediately became the benevolent uncle figure, bending down to lift the small boy into his arms as he spoke. And almost in the same instant a man and a woman, the former in western dress and the latter in a long, flowing jellaba but without a veil, appeared in the open doorway.

The following minutes of greetings and introductions took them into the house—which was as beautiful inside as out. It was wonderfully cool with its marbled floors and shaded inner courtyard complete with tinkling fountain and huge, leafy palms. Admiring their surroundings and making small talk with their hosts, and their small son, Abdul, eased the tension between her and Hudson.

Idris and his wife, Fatima, didn't appear to think it at all odd that Hudson had brought her along; in fact such was their open-handed hospitality and genuine delight that Marianne began to feel like an old friend, rather than a stranger in their midst.

'Have you known Hudson long?' She was sitting with Fatima on a long, low sofa in a shady part of the courtyard, sipping freshly squeezed orange juice flavoured with limes and lemon. The men had departed to Idris's study to see his new computer set-up, with Abdul still in Hudson's arms.

'Idris has known him since they were students together in the States,' Fatima answered quietly. 'But I first met Hudson on the day I married Idris, five years ago.'

'They seem very good friends,' Marianne observed, taking another sip of the deliciously cold drink. 'They're obviously very fond of each other.'

'This is true.' Fatima spoke perfect English with a quaint preciseness that was charming. 'Hudson helped Idris on the death of his first wife—you know Idris was married before?'

Marianne shook her head quickly. 'No, no, I didn't.'

'She was killed in an automobile accident,' Fatima said quietly, 'with their two children. The chauffeur also was killed. It was very hard for Idris, and Hudson—how do you say it?—dropped everything. Idris often says he does not know what he would have done if Hudson had not been there. He stayed with him many weeks. Hudson is a very compassionate man, yes?'

'Yes...' Compassionate? He might be; she really didn't know, Marianne thought numbly. Their whirlwind romance had lasted almost two months, and from the day they'd met they had barely been apart for more than a few hours. But...she hadn't got to know him—not really—not *properly*. It had been crazy, unreal—they had been locked into their own little world where everything had been vibrant and vivid and magical, and where one glance, one lingering look, had had the power to send her into the heavens. They had barely talked about their respective pasts, and the future had been nothing more than a rosy dream. It was the present that had been real, and they had known their immediate time together was limited.

Hudson had taken a three-month sabbatical from his law firm and had already used a month of that time before he had met her, and Marianne had had a new job waiting for her in Scotland. But on the night he had asked her to marry him—and she had accepted—she had known she would follow him anywhere. It had made the next few hours all the harder.

'Is it not...?'

'I'm sorry?' Marianne came to with a jolt to realise Fatima had been speaking and she hadn't heard a word. She blushed hotly, forcing herself to give all her attention to the Moroccan woman.

'I said your job must be very interesting, Marianne.' Fatima was too sensitive and far too well-bred to show open curiosity, but it was clear she was wondering where Marianne fitted into Hudson's life, and after a somewhat cagey conversation Marianne was relieved when the men returned and they all went through to the dining room to eat.

The meal was in traditional Moroccan style—everyone seated on sofas around a low table—and before they ate they were given towels and rose-water in order to wash their right hands—the hand Moroccans used to eat from the communal dishes they favoured. Marianne had heard of the custom, but only having eaten at the hotel—which was distinctly European—had never seen it in action.

She found it fascinating to watch the others reaching into a big bowl of couscous, picking up olives and raisins with three fingers, twirling them round in the creamy mixture and then popping them into their mouths. Normally she would have thoroughly enjoyed the experience—the table was full of mouth-watering dishes that smelt divine—but her stomach was so knotted with nerves, she could barely force anything past the constriction, and each mouthful was an effort of will.

Why had Hudson brought her here? The question was drumming in her head all through the meal and the subsequent conversation over coffee. She hadn't seen him for two years. They both had separate lives now—and if the tall, elegant redhead was anything to go by he hadn't exactly pined away for her, she thought with a touch of bitterness. He must hate her—he *did* hate her; he'd made that plain—so why bring her to his friend's home and act as though she was *with* him? Why put them both through such torment?

She didn't understand it and she didn't understand him, but he made her nervous—very nervous. She had never imagined he was a man who would forgive easily, but this—there was no rhyme or reason to it.

It was after eleven when they left Idris and Fatima, and the soft indigo dusk had given way to a black velvet sky pierced through with hundreds upon hundreds of bright, twinkling stars, the darkness perfumed with the heavy, rich scent of magnolia flowers.

It was a beautiful night—romantic, gentle, the full moon silhouetting the eastern horizon of flamboyant mosques and towering minarets with ethereal charm— but Marianne had never felt so tense and nervous in her life. Just sitting beside Hudson made her as jumpy as a cat on a hot tin roof, and she knew he sensed her agitation. Sensed it and was satisfied by it.

'You are frightened of me?' The dark, deep voice was silky-soft, but caused her to straighten her backbone as she glanced at the ruthlessly cold profile.

'Of course not,' she lied tightly, her voice cold and even.

'No?' The query was soft, charged with dark emotion.

'No.' She forced her hands, which had been clasped in tight fists on her lap, to relax before she said, her voice as steady and unemotional as she could make it, 'Why? Should I be?'

'Most certainly.' It wasn't the reply she had expected, and as her eyes widened with the shock of it her heart went haywire.

'You walked out on me, Annie, and no one had ever done that to me before. I didn't like it.' It was the understatement of the year, and delivered in such an expressionless voice that her blood flowed cold. 'I didn't like it at all.'

'I... I explained—'

'We had an agreement, Annie.' He continued as though she hadn't spoken. 'An agreement you welshed on. How do you think I should deal with that?' he asked coldly, his eyes on the road in front of them.

She stared at him warily, quite unable to gauge anything from the cool mask he could don at will and which proved so formidable in the courtroom. *He* was formidable, terrifyingly so.

'Now look, Hudson—'

'No, *you* look!' It was an explosion, hot and acidic, and as she felt herself shrink in the seat it dawned on her that he was furiously angry—that he had been furiously angry from that first moment of meeting her again. The fact that he had been holding the rage in didn't comfort her in the least, merely emphasising, as it did, the almost superhuman power and control he could exert over his emotions when he chose to do so. But the fury was still there, just waiting to escape the iron constraint and devour her, she thought shakily. And it had had two years to simmer and burn.

'You didn't seriously think I would just say hello and goodbye, did you?' he asked coldly. 'You owe me, Marianne McBride-Harding.'

'I owe you?' She was scared to death but she was blowed if he was going to bully her like this, and the sarcastic intonation of her name brought a welcome surge of angry adrenalin to melt the chill his intimidation had wrought on her psyche. 'Think again, Hudson,' she said tightly. 'I owe you nothing and you know it.'

'I've thought, Annie, I've thought long and hard,' he grated slowly. 'I've had two years to think, haven't I? Does the current boy wonder know what a cheating little liar you really are? Or are you stringing him along the way you did me?'

'Who...?' And then she realised. 'Keith? Keith is just my boss—' *Keith?* He seriously thought she was interested in Keith?

'And I'm Father Christmas,' Hudson said cuttingly.

'You don't believe me?' she asked hotly, aware that he was driving far too fast along the badly lit Moroccan roads but too angry to care. 'You think I'd lie just for the sake of it?'

'You find that surprising?' he rasped scathingly, his lips compressing in one straight, angry line. 'I believed you once, my faithless siren, but never again. This time the old adage once bitten, twice shy holds fast. Mind you—' he glanced at her, the movement lightning-fast but savage '—I think even you will be hard pressed to explain where you have been all evening.'

She stared at him, too stunned to reply as a hundred and one thoughts chased themselves through the turmoil of her mind. This had been a calculated exercise on his part, she told herself weakly, a cold-blooded, determined effort to make Keith think— Think what? she asked herself painfully as a sickening flood of desolation and despair washed over her. That she had been with Hudson in the biblical sense of the word—slept with him? Surely even Hudson wouldn't do that…? 'I shall simply tell him the truth,' she informed him through lips that were beginning to tremble.

'A novel experience for you, I'm sure,' he said mockingly. 'But you don't think he will find it a little…far-fetched? You accept a lift from a man you used to know—*years* ago,' he emphasised with a bitter twist to his lips, 'and then, instead of appearing bright-eyed and bushy-tailed as arranged, you are hours late. And the reason? You went to dinner with friends?' He shook his head slowly. 'Surely even this youthful-looking child will not accept such a story?' he asked with dark satisfaction.

'But it's true,' she protested angrily. 'You know it is.'

'I know it is. Idris and Fatima know it is.' The hard voice was merciless. 'But Keith will believe whatever I want him to believe. I met you by chance. I gave you a lift by chance. How could I have set up an evening such as you will describe?'

'Because…because your friend couldn't go with you to Idris's house, and you saw me and asked…' Her voice trailed away as he shook his black head slowly, his profile without mercy.

'I came to Tangier alone,' he said softly, 'as the hotel will confirm. You have no proof that there is a friend.'

'But I saw you with people this lunchtime.' In spite of the dire situation she couldn't bring herself to mention the redhead specifically. 'You *know* you were with— with them.'

'Pure chance.' His smile was without humour. 'Prove otherwise.'

'But you told Idris and Fatima you were bringing someone,' she insisted desperately. 'You *arranged* it with them.'

'Yes, I did.' A brief pause and then, 'But you do not know their surname, where they live, their telephone number. You will not be able to substantiate your story to the anxious Keith.'

'I shan't need to give proof.' She raised her head proudly. 'Keith will believe me,' she declared firmly.

'A man in love is a jealous man, Annie,' he said coolly. 'And jealous men are not reasonable at the best of times. And this…this will not be the best of times. Keith imagines he loves you.'

'You would lie?' she asked dazedly. 'You'd really do that?'

'Without hesitation.' It was immediate and cold.

'But I've told you, he isn't my boyfriend.' She glared at the imperturbable profile, her eyes fiery. 'It's all in your imagination.'

'Then you have no cause to worry that pretty little head, have you?' he said urbanely. 'All, as they say, is well.'

But it wasn't. A picture of Keith's face as it had been that lunchtime was suddenly there in front of her, and snippets of their conversation echoed in her mind. *He* had told *her* she wasn't over Hudson, at the same time as making it plain he cared about her. The way he had reacted to Hudson—his attitude towards her—it all confirmed her suspicions that Keith wanted more than just a working relationship.

'Don't ever try to play poker, Annie.' The voice was livid. 'And, as far as I'm concerned, I'm doing the guy a favour. At least he gets a warning, which is far more than I did.'

'It's not like that.' She had never wanted to hit someone so much in her life. 'I've *told* you, Keith and I are just friends.'

'Spare me.'

How could she hate someone, really hate them as she did Hudson at this minute, and yet love them so much it was a physical pain in her heart? Marianne asked herself bleakly as she settled back in her seat helplessly. And yet could she blame him for being like this? What would she have been like if the situation had been reversed and it had been Hudson who had walked out on her after that glorious two months they had shared? She would have wanted to kill him. It had been bad enough for her, knowing she *had* to go. But him...

She stared miserably through the dark windscreen as the car flashed swiftly through the black Moroccan night, her eyes blind.

She had been so happy when Hudson had asked her to marry him that night—ecstatic, wild with joy... She had known, from the first moment of meeting him, that there would never be anyone else for her, but that he'd felt the same had been too wonderful, too glorious to be true. He was an assured, astute man of the world, powerful, commanding, with a reputation that went before him to oil wheels and pave the way in a manner that had left her breathless. People held him in awe—not just for his wealth and formidable influence, but for the razor-sharp, ruthless intelligence that ravaged those foolish enough to try to deceive him.

He was incorruptible and totally honourable—and that

in a profession known for its subtle, and at times doubtful, elucidation of the law. He had his own moral code and he stuck to it—whatever pressure was brought to bear by colleagues or criminals. And he had loved *her*. It had seemed like a fairy tale, a dream, when he could have had any woman he wanted just by lifting his little finger. Beautiful, sophisticated, experienced women who would know all there was to know about pleasing a man.

She had mentioned Hudson in her letters home to her mother in Scotland, unable to hide her happiness, but had been less than pleased when her mother and stepfather had popped up in France the day before Hudson had asked her to marry him. Not that she hadn't been pleased to see her mother, but her stepfather...

Michael Caxton, an American living and working in Scotland for a big American company, had married her mother after a whirlwind courtship eighteen months before when Marianne had been at university, and from the first moment of meeting him after the marriage she had disliked him. He'd been too handsome, too charming—too much of everything. But her mother had loved him, and, having struggled on her own for five years after the death of Marianne's father, she had seized the chance of happiness with both hands.

So Marianne had kept her reservations to herself on her visits home, maintaining a surface civility whilst praying that her distrust and misgivings were unfounded. But they hadn't been, she reflected flatly.

Michael had still been up when she had got home on the night of Hudson's proposal—her mother, aunt and uncle having long since retired—and she had known somehow, as soon as she'd walked through the door, that his guise of being unable to sleep because of toothache was a lie. His eyes had been too sharp, too cunning.

'Nice evening?' It was deliberately casual.

'Yes, thank you.' She forced a smile whilst hoping she could escape with the minimum of conversation. He scared her.

'Getting on well with Hudson, are you?' he asked smoothly.

'Very well.' She looked straight at Michael then to find the pale blue eyes tight on her face. 'Do you know him?' she asked quietly as some sixth sense sent cold trickles down her spine. This was all about Hudson somehow; she felt it in her bones.

'I know *of* him.' Michael smiled but it didn't reach the unblinking orbs, and she realised then, as a warning bell began to clang stridently in her brain, that his smiles never did. His eyes were the eyes of a shark—empty, cold, dead... 'Oh, yes, I certainly know of him. He's a one-man vigilante for law and order in the States, an advocate for the all-American way.'

'Well, that's good, surely?' she replied warily, the fierce joy and excitement that had carried her into the house on wings beginning to die. 'We need order and laws, don't we?'

'Probably...for the masses,' Michael drawled slowly. 'Those content to be led all their lives, who want nothing more than a paltry monthly pay cheque that enables them to scrape through to the next month.' It was clear he didn't put himself in that category.

'And you're not like that?' She suddenly would have given the world to step back in time an hour and not be there. She was going to hear something she didn't want to hear; the hairs that were standing up on the back of her neck told her so. 'You're different?'

'How do you think I bought the place in Scotland, Marianne?'

Michael had been living in a hotel when he'd first met her mother, but a few weeks before the wedding he had bought what virtually amounted to a small castle, complete with acres of grounds housing a lake, deer—and had taken great delight in acting the feudal lord.

'I don't know,' she said quietly. 'I haven't thought about it.'

'Use your imagination.' And then as she still stared

at him with great, accusing eyes, he snapped, 'And don't look at me like that, damn you. You either make it or you don't in this world—there are only two choices— and to make it you take all the help you can get. I've...done favours for people, bent the rules a little, oiled wheels,' he finished softly, his eyes narrowed and hard.

'But you're an accountant,' she murmured naively. 'How—?'

'Hudson is going to get offered a case in the next little while, and if he takes it it could prove...uncomfortable for people who have been very good to me. If the dirt starts to fly it'll come my way too, and a little bit of dirt contaminates everything it comes into contact with— your mother, you—and if you're with Hudson...'

'What...what case?' she asked through numb lips.

'Things have been hotting up for some time, but eighteen months ago certain people decided I'd better leave the States and lie low—subpoenas have a nasty habit of rearing their heads when you least expect them,' he continued almost matter-of-factly.

'Does my mother know?' She couldn't believe the conversation was really taking place, not here, in her aunt's pretty little sitting room. 'Does she know why you left the States?'

'Of course not. I never discuss my business with anyone,' he drawled softly, his voice at odds with the intensity of the chillingly cold eyes. 'It is...personal.'

'Then why are you telling me?' she asked bewilderedly.

'Think, girl, think!' The words were harsh before he collected himself and continued in the same soft tone as before, 'It is clear from what you've told your mother that you have some influence with Hudson de Sance, and that is a bonus we could never have arranged if we had tried for years. If de Sance doesn't take the case it will come to nothing, end of story.' He smiled meaningfully.

'You're asking me to persuade him not to take it?'

she asked numbly. 'Is that what this is all about? You expect me to do that?'

'Exactly.' Now the soft voice was persuasive. 'It will be best for everyone concerned—you see that, surely? Me, your mother, you—even Hudson. It will not do his sterling reputation any good when it comes to light he's having an affair with the daughter of one of the men he's prosecuting. And it *would* come to light…'

'*I am not your daughter,*' she shot back bitterly.

'The media won't see it like that,' he countered darkly.

'And it's not an affair, not like you mean. He…he wants me to marry him,' she said desperately. 'He loves me.'

'Does he? Does he indeed…?' Michael nodded reflectively. 'Better and better.'

'I hate you.' She glared at him, her eyes blazing. 'You married my mother purely as a cover, didn't you? And you'll dump her as soon as it suits you. You don't love her; you're incapable of love. I bet you couldn't believe your luck when I began to date Hudson—'

'A gift from the lap of the gods,' he confirmed sardonically. 'And definitely not to be ignored. Now, if you're clever, Marianne, you'll use this for your own advantage. I can make you a very wealthy woman in your own right, and as Hudson's wife…'

'Even if I agreed to this, it wouldn't be just this one time, would it?' she said bitterly. 'You'd put Hudson in a terrible position, use emotional blackmail about me and my mother, threaten to blacken his name through me if he didn't agree to what you and your friends want. He would never be free of you.'

'It would be just this once; you have my word,' he said smoothly, but she saw the look in his eyes and knew she was right.

'Your word?' she repeated scathingly. 'You're despicable, filthy. I can't bear that my mother has allowed you to touch her.'

'Careful, Marianne, be very careful,' he warned silkily. 'I can break her and I can break you, and my friends have extensive influence. Just be sensible and all this can be worked out very nicely.'

But she didn't behave according to Michael's definition of sensible. She escaped to her room and sat there for hours, her mind desperately seeking a release from the horror, only to come to the conclusion that there wasn't one. She couldn't put Hudson through the torment that her revelation would involve—whichever course of action he took. Either he compromised everything he had built his life, character and reputation around—and Michael would make sure he kept on compromising, too—or he would have to fight her stepfather and his criminal friends, and in the process, through his relationship with her, mud would stick to him, too. It was a no-win situation whichever way she looked at it.

Unless she left Hudson now. Disappeared out of his life. Disappeared out of everyone's life. Her heart pounded furiously, but it was the only way.

She wrote three letters. One to her mother, explaining everything. One to Michael, informing him she was going where no one would find her and that she was telling Hudson nothing except that their relationship was over. And one—the most difficult—to Hudson. And then she packed, left the house before dawn, and once in England made for London, her mind and emotions shattered.

She couldn't remember much now about the first few months, although she had survived somehow—living in a tiny bedsit and working as a waitress, her mind on automatic most of the time. Later she'd realised she had had some sort of mini-breakdown, but at the time she had just got through each day as it came, the blackness in her soul absolute.

The thing that had shocked her out of the stupor was seeing an old friend from her home village purely by chance, and learning in the middle of a crowded café that her mother and Michael were dead, killed in a car

crash the day after they had returned to Scotland. It had
been like a blow straight between the eyes.

She had grieved desperately for her mother, hated Michael with a vengeance that had shocked her, longed for
Hudson with renewed intensity. But gradually, over the
following weeks, she had come to the realisation that
she was thinking and feeling and living again—even if
the main element to it all was suffering. Agonising suffering.

'Would you like me to hold your hand while you face
the music?'

'What?' The dark, silky voice had intruded into the
nightmare world with all the softness of cold steel, but
as she came out of her reverie she saw her hotel looming
up in the distance and a new sort of panic rose. 'Oh, no,
I don't; of course I don't,' she snapped testily—hating
him, loving him, feeling as though she couldn't take
much more without howling like a baby.

'He might wonder why you didn't phone him to tell
him where you were,' Hudson suggested quietly. 'I wondered that myself. Why didn't you?' The grey eyes
flashed her way for one vital second.

Because it simply hadn't occurred to her, she thought
helplessly. She hadn't thought of Keith once, not once,
through the evening; all her thoughts and emotions had
been tied up with the tall, ruthless man at her side. 'It
wasn't necessary,' she said stiffly. 'I don't answer to
Keith or anyone else.'

'Hmm, independent, eh?' he drawled easily. 'Funny,
I don't remember you as quite so militant when you were
with me.'

She wasn't militant, she was melted jelly inside,
Marianne thought with painful self-awareness; but the
time had long since passed when she could have explained her actions to him. Perhaps if she had known
about Michael's death when it had happened—had gone
to Hudson then and told him everything—things might
have been different now. But then again Michael's un-

timely death hadn't negated any of her reasons for leaving Hudson. The contact with her would still have been there; the people Michael had been involved with could still have tried to discredit Hudson through her. Whichever way she had looked there had still been no solution.

When she had found out about the car crash she had contacted the family solicitor, and had been amazed to find Michael and her mother had left everything to her in a will they'd made when they had married. Michael's wealth had been considerable, and she would never forget the absolute shock and amazement on the solicitor's face when she had insisted on giving everything she had inherited to charity. But to her it had been blood money—tainted, unclean—and she had only been able to breathe freely again when every last penny had gone, even though part of it had been from her mother's estate.

'Here we are. And look who's waiting like an anxious mother hen,' Hudson said softly, and nastily, as the sports car growled to a stop outside the hotel and Hudson cut the powerful engine.

Marianne looked, and then felt a pang of deep and mortifying guilt as she saw Keith's worried face—which was made all the worse by the knowledge that Hudson's cruel analogy wasn't far off beam.

'I suppose a goodnight kiss is out of the question?' Hudson drawled with mocking amusement, his good humour apparently restored at the sight of Keith practically dancing in agitation as he raced down the steps towards them.

'You're a rotten swine,' she hissed furiously.

'I know...' His voice carried a wealth of satisfaction.

As Keith reached them and opened the passenger door Hudson left the driver's seat to stand just outside the car, his brawny arms leaning on the top of the vehicle as he watched Marianne alight.

'Where have you been?' Keith's voice was several octaves higher than normal, his round, boyish face flushed and perspiring. 'I expected you to be here when

I got back this afternoon, and then I thought you'd at
least be back for dinner.'

'I'm sorry—' Marianne began quickly, but the tirade
continued.

'I've been worried to death, and none of the others
knew where you were.' He was ignoring Hudson as
though the big figure watching them with such obvious
satisfaction didn't exist. 'Couldn't you have phoned or
something? Just a few words to say where you were?'

'It was my fault, I'm afraid.' Hudson's voice was like
smooth cream, and even a babe in arms would have been
able to tell he was enjoying every minute. 'We…had
dinner with some friends.'

How could he make the truth sound so much like a
lie? Marianne thought savagely. He'd done that on purpose—that brief pause which had made what followed
sound even more unlikely. Oh, she hated him!

'Isn't that so, Annie?' He made the pet name take on
soft and unbelievable connotations as he shifted his big
body lazily, his eyes glittering in the muted light from
the hotel.

'Yes, yes, it is.' Well, it *was*. 'They…these friends of
Hudson's had prepared us a meal,' she continued helplessly as Keith drew back slightly, disbelief written all
over his face. 'It—it would have been rude…I—I
couldn't really leave,' she stammered.

'And they didn't have a phone?' Keith asked tightly.

Oh, she wished he'd leave this until they were alone
and she could explain properly, Marianne thought desperately, vitally aware of the entertainment value the little tableau was affording Hudson. Couldn't Keith see he
was playing right into the other man's hands? Apparently he couldn't.

'Well? *Did* they have a phone?' Keith repeated snap-
pily.

'I…I don't know.' She stared at him unhappily.
'Can't we discuss this inside?' she suggested quietly.
'Please, Keith?'

'Yes, they have a phone.' The deep voice spoke again from the other side of the car. 'We just didn't think of it, I'm afraid. Enjoying ourselves too much, I guess,' Hudson added smoothly.

She'd hit him. She would—she'd hit him. Marianne took a deep breath and prayed for calm. 'Keith, I really can explain—'

'We are shooting at five tomorrow morning, Marianne, and I would appreciate you being in the lobby at half past four.' Keith had drawn himself up to his full five feet nine inches, quivering hot outrage in every line of his pink face. 'It is important we catch the dawn light, so don't be late,' he added sharply.

'No, of course I won't, but if I could just explain—'

'Goodnight, Marianne.' He strode back into the hotel without looking back, his back stiff and his head upright.

'Now look what you've done!' She rounded on Hudson like a small virago. 'I've never seen him like that. How *could* you?'

'Easily; the man's a fool,' Hudson said drily. 'Hasn't he heard of the concept of fighting for what he wants? Or has everything dropped into his lap so readily he's nothing more than spoonfed? Faint heart never won fair lady, and all that.'

'You know nothing about Keith.' She was angry, furiously angry, at his arrogance. 'He's a lovely man— gentle, good-natured—'

'So is the average cocker spaniel,' he returned coolly, and in her rage she didn't notice how his mouth had thinned with her championship of the other man. 'But the attributes that make a pet dog so worthy would soon pall in a lover, believe me.'

'He is *not* my lover!' she spat heatedly. 'He never has been.'

'He'd like to be.' It was straight for the jugular, and so true she was lost for an answer. 'And you know it,' he added grimly as her fiery face spoke for itself. 'So cut the twaddle.'

'Is that why you behaved like this tonight?' she asked hotly. 'Because you know——?' She could have kicked herself for the slip, and continued quickly, 'Because you think he loves me?'

'I think he *imagines* he's in love with you,' Hudson answered cynically. 'Which is quite a different thing, as we both know. He doesn't know you any more than I knew you—he loves the fantasy you project, like I did. With me, I guess it provided a kick to the holiday for you to have a little fling before you returned home to your fiancé, yes? With him, no doubt, it's good to have the boss panting for you—gives you the edge over the rest of the girls.'

'You're disgusting,' she bit out tightly, masking the pain and crucifying hurt his words had caused with superhuman effort.

'Realistic is the word.' He surveyed her coldly with dark, narrowed eyes, his black hair and the shadowed planes and angles of his face bleak in the moonlight. 'Yes, I'm realistic about you now, Annie. I only get taken for a ride once; you'd better understand that.'

'I didn't take you for a ride,' she protested shakily. 'It wasn't like that.' She stared at him helplessly, her mouth tremulous.

'No? Then what do you call it when you agree to marry one man, knowing there's already another tucked away back home you're promised to?' he spat out menacingly. 'Tell me; I'd really like to know.'

'It wasn't true, what Michael told you.' She stared at him, her green-gold eyes reflecting a shaft of moonlight that turned her hair silver. 'He had no right to say what he did.'

'Wasn't true?' He laughed harshly. 'Oh, come on, Annie, don't disappoint me now; you can do better than that.'

'It wasn't,' she insisted quietly. 'I'm telling you the truth.'

'Then what was true? That ''goodbye, Hudson, thanks

for the memories but I've decided the life of a lawyer's wife is not for me'' letter you left for me?' he asked grimly. 'You're telling me that you just got cold feet, that that was the reason you disappeared off the face of the earth for I don't know how long? Do I look stupid, Annie? Do I?' he added savagely, his face dark and cold.

How could she tell him? She stared at him as her mind raced. If she told him the truth, the whole truth, he could react one of three ways. It was clear he didn't love her any more, so he might just acknowledge what she said and walk away.

Or—and here her heart thudded—he might pity her, feel some responsibility towards her, especially if he guessed she still loved him, and ask her to take up where they left off in spite of the fact his feelings had died. If he did that, would the threat to him through her still remain? Probably, she thought grimly. From what she had heard, the sort of people Michael had been involved with had very long memories. And then the last two years would have been for nothing.

Or, thirdly—and she had to admit most likely—he simply wouldn't believe her anyway; he would think she was making up some fantastic story to cover her deceit. And with Michael's death all chance of proving what she had to say was gone. Hudson was far more likely to believe her stepfather's lies—he had had two years to let Michael's lie work its poison.

There was every reason for saying nothing and none for telling him the truth, except... Except she couldn't bear him to look at her with such contempt and scorn. She swallowed the lump in her throat. She had missed him so much, so much, and she didn't know what to do about it...

'Don't bother trying to work out what to say.' He slid back into the car as he spoke, his voice hard. 'I wouldn't believe it anyway.' The driver's door shut with a savageness that was very final.

Well, that settled her answer. She watched him for a

moment with misty eyes as he drove the car over to the small car park surrounded by bushes and flowering vegetation. He despised her, and she really couldn't blame him. Perhaps if she told him the truth he wouldn't believe she and her mother had had no knowledge of Michael's involvement in such heavy crime anyway. He had fought such people all his working life and loathed them and the corruption they represented. Maybe him thinking she had been hiding a fiancé in the background was light in comparison.

She turned quickly as the lights on the car died, walking swiftly into the hotel and picking up the key to her room before Hudson reappeared; knowing she couldn't face him again that night. But perhaps he was finished with her anyway? He'd made his point, told her exactly what he thought of her and in what contempt he held her; perhaps he would be satisfied with that? She had hurt him, she knew that—the knowledge had sent her half mad at times—but the alternative would have been far worse; it could have destroyed him and his career, she told herself frantically.

She reached her room, entering it quickly and then leaning weakly back against the door in the darkness as the tears began to seep from her closed eyelids. She had done the only thing she could two years ago, and it had been because she loved him, pure and simple. So why couldn't she gain just the smallest crumb of comfort from the knowledge to help combat the pain that was tearing her apart inside? It wasn't fair; none of this was fair.

She sank to the floor, her legs finally giving way as the storm of weeping overtook her, her moans like the cries of a wounded animal that had no hope.

She had just been learning to live without him, to accept that her life would never be one of fulfilment in the family sense—as a wife and mother—and now the pain was as raw and lacerating as it ever had been in the early days.

How long she lay there she didn't know, but when at last she rose, her face sticky and damp, there were no more tears left—only a cold, chilling emptiness in the pit of her stomach as she recalled his last words to her and the look on his face as he had uttered them.

CHAPTER THREE

'WHAT'S the matter with Keith today?' Marjorie pulled
a face as she bent over Marianne and whispered in her
ear, 'He's like a bear with a sore head; I've never seen
him like this. Is it because you were late back last night?'

'I don't think that helped,' Marianne said quietly as
the wafer-thin model straightened again, and they both
looked to where Keith was bawling at June and Guy, his
face turkey-red.

'He makes my Tony seem like a positive angel,'
Marjorie drawled softly. 'And that's hard to do, believe
me. Well, we live and learn. I had no idea Keith had it
in him.' She glanced down at Marianne again, who was
setting up the equipment, her face pale and sombre.
'He's crazy about you, you know,' she added quietly.

'Marjorie, please...' Marianne raised anguished eyes.
'That doesn't help. I could never think of Keith in that
way.'

'Sorry.' There was a pause, and then, 'Mind you, if I
had the choice of Keith or that hunk you went off with
yesterday there'd be no contest. He was absolutely *gorgeous*. Old flame?'

'Sort of.' Marianne's voice was dismissive but it
didn't work.

'You were careless to let that one escape,' Marjorie
said softly, her beautiful almond-shaped eyes bright with
curiosity. 'Is he married? The best ones usually are,' she
added resignedly.

'Marjorie, I've got to do this.' Marianne kept her head
bent to the task in hand. 'Okay?'

'I get the message: mind your own business,
Marjorie,' the other girl said good-naturedly. 'But if he's

not married and you want to introduce us…?' she whee-
dled hopefully.

'It was a one-off, Marjorie; I probably shan't be seeing him again,' Marianne said as calmly as she could
through her screaming nerves. Much more of this and
she would say something she'd regret.

'Pity.' The model sighed deeply. 'Great, great pity.'

The morning had started badly and got progressively
worse, and by lunchtime Keith's bad temper had affected
everyone, making the very air tense and volatile, which
made it all the more awkward when, just as they were
packing up, Marjorie called across, 'Marianne, you know
that one-off? He's going for double.'

'What?' She straightened and turned as she spoke, and
then froze, her heartbeat going haywire, as she saw the
tall, dark figure watching them from the road as he leant
indolently against the side of his car, his hands thrust
into the pockets of his jeans and sunglasses hiding his
eyes. How could one man look so—so *gorgeous*?

They had been filming on Tangier's three-mile-long
white sandy beach, the atmosphere enhanced by several
grazing camels and the two barefoot, curly-haired
Moroccan children tending the animals; they had been
delighted to pose for the cameras for a few dirhams.
Although the May sun had been pleasantly warm at first,
for the last two hours it had been blazing down out of
a cloudless blue sky with the temperature steadily soar-
ing. Marianne felt hot and dirty and sticky, and the last
person—the very last person in all the world—she
wanted to see at that moment was Hudson de Sance.

'Did you arrange to meet him here?' Keith had moved
to her side when Marjorie had drawn everyone's attention to the brooding figure watching them so intently,
and now Marianne turned to look at the slight
Englishman, rubbing her hand across her damp forehead
as she did so. This was all she needed—Keith throwing
a wobbly.

'No.' She had a thudding headache, she was tired, and

she had never felt more like a bone between two bridling dogs, and she was blowed if she was going to explain further. She'd had enough.

'Do you want to talk to him?' Keith asked stiffly, his nose, cheeks and forehead scarlet from the sun and his thin, stringy legs, in the wide khaki shorts he was wearing, boyishly innocuous.

No, she didn't want to talk to him, but when did someone not wanting to do something ever stop Hudson de Sance if *he* wanted it? she asked herself grimly. 'Not particularly, but it will be easier in the long run,' she said flatly, watching his shrug and angry grimace as he flounced away with a stab of very real irritation before guilt swamped her.

He was only behaving like this because he liked her, she told the little voice in her mind that had pointed out—with devastating and clear honesty—that Hudson would never behave so petulantly and childishly. She could imagine Hudson being coldly sarcastic with a supposed rival, perhaps even aggressive if he thought the occasion warranted it, but indulging in the tantrums and querulous, peevish behaviour they had been forced to endure that morning? Never. It simply wasn't in his nature, she admitted silently.

She tried to ignore her crumpled, grubby appearance as she slowly walked over the hot, powdery sand towards the road, but it was a little difficult, especially as she could see, the nearer she got, that Hudson was his normal impeccable self—his jet-black hair slicked off a forehead that was tanned a deep golden brown and his short-sleeved dark blue shirt crisp and crease-free.

'You've been working hard, I see.' It could have meant anything, spoken as it had been in an expressionless drawl and with the lethal, piercing grey eyes hidden behind dark glass, but she bristled instantly, feeling it was a comment on her appearance.

'Yes.' It was a snap, and she tried to moderate her

tone as she continued, 'Did you want to see me?' It was a stupid question.

His voice acknowledged the fact as he said, 'How intuitive of you.'

It would have been better if they had never met again, she thought miserably, than for them to be reduced to this cold war of words. She could understand him hating her; the letter itself had been bad enough, but after what Michael had told him...

She was unaware her shoulders had slumped wearily with her thoughts, or that her face was pale with exhaustion under the big straw hat she had pulled on as protection against the fierce Moroccan sun, so when he said, his voice soft, 'Have you finished here?' she looked at him warily, mistrusting the sudden mellowing.

'Why?' she asked suspiciously, her back straightening.

'Just a yes or no will suffice.'

'It probably would, but it's not as simple as that,' she said testily. 'We can't work through the heat of the afternoon, but Keith wants to take some shots of the girls in evening wear later when the sun begins to set and it's a few degrees cooler.'

'So you are finished for the moment,' he stated quietly. 'Good. In that case you can accept a lift back to the hotel with me.' The dark eyebrows quirked as he smiled mockingly.

It was said so tongue-in-cheek, it wasn't meant to be taken seriously, and she frowned at him as she said, her voice tart, 'And how long would it take this time?'

'A drive-and-a-picnic long?' he drawled easily, completely unabashed by her fierceness. 'The goodies are all on board.'

'I don't think so.' She glared at him, more to hide the thudding of her heart and the sudden weakness in her legs than anything else. He had sought her out again—for whatever reason.

'You'd prefer me to carry you off kicking and screaming?' he asked casually. 'Is that wise?'

'You wouldn't dare.' She glanced quickly over her shoulder to the others, her gaze taking in the long stretch of beach dotted here and there with holiday-makers intent on making the most of the sun, along with the ever hopeful vendors of knick-knacks made of ornamental brass and copper, and others selling rugs and leather goods.

'No? Try me.' It was cool and threatening. 'You think your boyfriend would try to rescue you from the dragon?' he continued sardonically. 'Funny, but I don't see that guy as a white knight myself.'

'I don't know why you are doing this,' she said shakily, 'but even you must see it's pointless. Anything between us was finished two years ago—you admitted that yourself last night—'

'Wrong.' He straightened against the car as he spoke, removing the sunglasses so the full force of the deadly grey gaze was exposed, his eyes cold and glittering in the golden sunshine. 'You walked out on an agreement, Annie, and in my book that makes it far from finished,' he said levelly. 'Now, are you going to tell that bozo that you're occupied this afternoon, or do I have to do it?'

'I will.' He was right; they had to get this sorted out once and for all—she owed him that at least. But she couldn't tell him the truth, so she would have to lie—again. And she had been foolish last night, very foolish, in contesting Michael's fabrication about another man. He hadn't believed her, but it had been enough to get that formidable lawyer's brain ticking over—which was probably why he was here today, she told herself wretchedly.

It had been weakness on her part, because she couldn't bear him to think ill of her when he was here, face to face, in front of her, but he had to. It was the only way and she knew it. There was no future for them—there never had been; anything they might have shared had been dealt a fatal blow eighteen months before she'd met him when her mother had married Michael. Any lawyer's wife—but especially Hudson de Sance's—couldn't have the slightest shadow hanging over her reputation or credibility. If she had stayed with him then she would have been a millstone round his neck, dragging him down. And nothing had changed. However much she wished it had.

Keith was straight-faced and tight-lipped when she explained she was going for a drive with Hudson, but, in view of the fact he had told them all earlier they had the afternoon off, he couldn't very well object. Nevertheless, he made her feel incredibly guilty, yet again, as she left the others—Marjorie slipping in a sly wink and thumbs-up sign when Keith wasn't looking—and returned to the car.

It wasn't fair, she told herself silently as she reached the road. She had never, in all the months she had been working for him, encouraged this attention by so much as a word or gesture he could misconstrue. In fact for the last little while in particular she had tactfully made it clear—on numerous occasions—that she wasn't interested in anything of a personal nature.

'Didn't like it much, did he?' Hudson's deep voice couldn't hide his satisfaction—not that he tried to, Marianne thought nastily—and she glared at him angrily as she settled herself in the passenger seat of the beautiful sports car.

'Is that why you asked me? To get under Keith's skin?' she snapped accusingly. 'I consider that pathetic in the extreme.'

'Would I?' The wicked grey eyes were laughing at her, which made her all the madder. How could he get under her skin so quickly?

'You know darn well you would,' she bit back sharply.

'Annie, your lack of faith in the nobleness of my actions is like a sword-thrust into the heart.' He eyed her mockingly.

She said something rude which surprised them both, and then clapped her hand over her mouth as she turned bright pink. 'Oh, you *horrible* man...'

'Er, excuse me, but it was you who just swore, and very succinctly too, I might add,' Hudson murmured drily, his mouth curving as he noted her distress. 'I don't know who has been teaching you such dreadful phrases, but if we weren't so far from the hotel I'd take you back and wash out your mouth with soap and water,' he added with righteous disapproval.

'I don't normally... I mean...' She was floundering, and if it hadn't been for the fact that she looked as though she was going to burst into tears he would have let her continue for a little while longer.

'Relax, Annie, I've heard a lot worse,' he said softly, unable to keep all amusement out of his voice. He worked with women who could utter the most extreme profanities without turning a hair, let alone blush at the mild swear word she had uttered.

That had been one of the things that had bowled him over two years ago—her gentle innocence in a world that he knew, only too well, was neither gentle nor innocent. Only she hadn't been, had she? All amusement fled as the thought hammered home. She'd played him for a sucker and then calmly walked away when things had got too hot. *She'd chosen the other man over him.*

He felt the red-hot rage that always accompanied such thoughts grip his mind and shoot down to his stomach, causing powerful muscles to clench and contract as he fought the anger.

And then she had disappeared—so completely that even he, with all his contacts, legitimate and otherwise, had been unable to find her. How long had she been with this other guy? And what had gone wrong with the marriage plans? Had he dumped her? Was that it? Or had she got bored with him too? *Damn her...*

'How long are you staying in Tangier?'

Her voice brought him back from the darkness but it took a moment or two for him to get control sufficiently to reply, his voice cool and hard, 'As long as it takes to complete my business here.' It was cold and succinct, and certainly not a prelude to further conversation.

'Oh.' It wasn't really an answer but the temperature had dropped about twenty degrees since she had got into the car, and she couldn't nerve herself to say anything more.

It was another twenty minutes before Marianne spoke again, and then simply because the silent, brooding mood within the car had brought her to screaming pitch and she couldn't bear it a minute more without breaking.

And Hudson would just love that, she thought bitterly as she turned to glance at the dark, handsome face that had been at the forefront of her mind for two years. He was a brilliant strategist—as many an outwitted and broken criminal would testify—and when that attribute was added to a razor-sharp brain and ruthless determination it made him an adversary to be reckoned with. And that was what she was now to him, she reflected miserably—an adversary. It was as cold-blooded as that.

'How long will it take? To...to get where we're going?' she asked quietly. 'You do realise I can't go too far?'

'Worried?' His tone wasn't pleasant and neither was his face.

'Worried?' She forced a laugh that wasn't as confident as she would have liked. 'Don't be ridiculous; of course I'm not worried. But I have to get back for the shoot this evening, that's all. I happen to be working out here, in case you haven't noticed.'

'I'll deliver you back in good time, Annie, never fear,' he drawled mockingly. 'But in the meantime what could be more pleasant than two old friends enjoying some time together?' He glanced at her and his smile was one of hard, satisfied contempt as he saw the fiery colour flood her face. 'We're going to one of the larger weekly markets, actually; it was recommended as worth seeing by a friend of mine,' he continued expressionlessly. 'But we'll stop in a moment and have a bite to eat. You look in need of sustenance.' The last comment was very dry.

What he really meant was that she looked like something the cat had dragged in, Marianne thought unhappily, resisting the impulse to reach forward and peer into the little mirror above her head. She knew that already—she didn't need Hudson de Sance to rub it in, especially with him looking as cool as a cucumber.

She knew what he wanted from this meeting—to dot the i's and cross the t's with regard to any question marks he might still have about her abrupt departure two years ago. That formidable lawyer's brain wouldn't rest until it was satisfied.

But oh—she caught her breath as a shaft of pain so acute as to be paralysing speared through her—how could she say what she *had* to say when she still loved him so much? The last two years had been a day-by-day exercise in quelling all emotion and dealing ruthlessly with any weakness her feelings induced, and she had thought, foolishly, that she was beginning to win. But the moment she had seen him again she had known she was as smitten as ever—more, if possible, she corrected bitterly. She should have known you didn't recover from falling in love with Hudson—it was an incurable disease. She shut her eyes briefly and prayed for strength.

They ate in the shade of a little oasis of eucalyptus trees some way from the road, the air hot and heavy and quite silent. She didn't ask from where he had obtained the small picnic-basket full of mouthwatering delicacies, or the deliciously iced fruit drink that was so thirst-quenching—all her energy and resources were taken up with telling herself she had to be strong against the insidious attraction of the man watching her so intently.

'You can take the hat off now.' He had been lying on one elbow for some minutes on the thick blanket he had brought from the car, and now he reached over to where she was sitting and tweaked the big straw hat off her head, taking her completely by surprise.

'Don't!' She made a grab for the inoffensive article, painfully aware that the neat, cool knot on top of her head that had been so tidy early that morning was now in tumultuous disarray, but he was too quick for her.

'It's shady here.' The grey eyes skimmed the cascade of pale golden curls that had worked loose from the severe restraint to tumble in silken strands about her neck and cheeks. 'You might as well take those grips and things out,' he suggested softly. 'Most of your hair is down already.'

'I don't want to,' she snapped hotly, knowing she must look as though she had been dragged through a hedge backwards. 'And may I have my hat back, please?' she asked severely.

'No.' Suddenly he was grinning at her, and she could have hit him as he continued, 'It's a monstrosity of a hat, and doesn't do a thing for you. You were never meant to wear hats, Annie.'

'The only thing I wanted it to do for me was to keep my head covered, and it did that quite well,' she retorted tightly. 'Now, if you don't mind...?' She glared at him as she held out her hand.

'I do mind.' He rolled closer so that he was almost touching her, and smiled up at her derisively as she stiffened. 'I mind very much. I like seeing your hair loose, like a cloud of spun gold. You used to wear it like that all the time in the old days.'

'It's not suitable when I'm working,' she said primly.

'You aren't working now,' he reminded her softly.

She stared down at him, a mixture of fear and excitement making her as stiff as a board and the clean, fresh male fragrance that emanated from his skin causing her stomach muscles to tighten until it hurt. He was dangerous, he was so dangerous, and she should have known better than to come with him like this...

'You're even more beautiful than you were two years ago,' he murmured huskily. 'How have you managed that, Annie? To grow in beauty and femininity when you're so rotten inside? There's no justice...'

Before she realised what was happening, he had pulled her down beside him and moved over her in one continuous, fluid movement, his body covering hers as he trapped her beneath him, his weight resting on his elbows. 'I don't want to want you but I do,' he continued almost thoughtfully, the rapid pulse in his throat belying the controlled voice. 'And I don't like that...weakness at all.'

'Hudson, stop this; let me go.' She didn't dare struggle, vitally aware of the big, powerful body covering hers and of the alien masculinity. 'I don't want this.'

'How many times did you make love with him, Annie? The one you left me for?' he asked grimly. 'And how many were there after him? How many were there *before*, if it comes to that?' he added tightly. 'Was I the only one who didn't have you? The only one who believed you when you said you wanted to wait until we were married? Did the others see you for what you are?'

She stared at his face, inches from hers. 'Let me go, *now*.'

'You know how to turn a man on; there's no doubt about that.' He looked down at her, his eyes glittering black and fierce in the tanned darkness of his face. 'And we came so close at times; do you remember?' He lowered himself slightly, his body stirring over hers as his fingers entwined themselves in the silky tangle of her hair. 'But you wanted to be married in white, you wanted it to mean something.' His sudden bark of a laugh was harsh and savage. 'Would it still mean something, Annie?' he asked bitterly.

A separate portion of her mind that wasn't taken up with the angry male body dominating hers was aware of the vivid blue of the sky above, the quiet, dusty vista beyond the shade of the eucalyptus trees, the still, sluggish air and the lightning movements of small, flat, large-eyed lizards who were darting back and forth just beyond the edge of the blanket, searching for crumbs from the picnic, and it made what was happening all the more unreal.

'You seemed so young then, so unsure and gentle and dreamy-eyed,' he mused softly. 'I had the feeling I had to treat you like fragile porcelain, that I mustn't frighten you in any way by rushing you. I was so conscious I was years older than you—not just numerically but in the ways of the world.' He paused, and then, 'How you must have laughed at me, Annie,' he added with sinister control, his face darkening and his mouth a thin, hard line.

'No, no, I didn't,' she protested shakily, terrified of what he was going to do. 'It wasn't like that; you know it wasn't.'

'Did you tell him all about me? Laugh about me together?' he asked menacingly. 'The ruthless and cynical Hudson de Sance fooled by a little slip of an English girl?'

'No, I told you, it wasn't like that,' she repeated desperately.

'What *was* it like, then?' he bit back savagely. 'Tell me, Annie. I'd really like to know, to understand.'

There it was again, that blindingly brilliant lawyer's brain that couldn't bear to think it hadn't sensed or known what was beneath its nose, she thought despairingly. That was what this was all about at root level. He was over her—of course he was—men like Hudson didn't wait two years for anyone. But her supposed deceit that had fooled him so completely was still rankling like a festering sore in that stunningly intelligent mind.

She began to struggle but stopped almost instantly, her twisting only making her aware of the hard and powerful male lines of his big frame as she came into intimate contact with his body. And there was something else she was hotly, and humiliatingly, aware of too—she wanted him desperately. If he began to make love to her it wouldn't be rape. And then he proved that very point.

He bent his head, his mouth hard on hers, possessive, his hands clasping either side of her head as she tried to turn her face away and his body touching the length of her. She tried—she really, really tried—to hide what effect he was having on her shaky equilibrium but it was useless: the moment their mouths had fused it had been fire meeting fire. She was lost, utterly lost.

In the old days, when he had first met her, his lovemaking had been warm and coaxing in deference to her innocence, and later, even when he'd asked her to marry him, she had always sensed he was exercising an enormous control over his desire for her, his demands always tempered by the knowledge of her youth. Now there was no such restraint.

His mouth was heated as it plundered hers, demanding its right to probe and explore, and as sensation shot through every part of her body she could feel herself melting for him, becoming fluid and soft and moist. She wanted to draw back, to tell him that this was wrong, that *he* was wrong, that she wasn't the accomplished lover and woman of the world he seemed to think she was, but she couldn't. His lips and hands wouldn't let her.

He moved his body over hers in a deliberate fuelling of her passion as he kissed her, and although she could hear the soft little moans of desire that were whimpering in her throat she was unable to stem them, her will to resist quite gone.

'You want me, Annie. In spite of everything you want me.' His voice was soft and husky against her lips, but there was a note of triumph there too that she recognised with a little jolt of her heart. This was premeditated, she told herself frantically—a cold-blooded exercise on his part to show her he only had to touch her and the old magic was as powerful as it had ever been.

But he wanted her badly—that much was genuine, as

his body was showing her only too clearly, his arousal huge. Yes, he wanted her—in a physical sense. But the essence of his previous relationship with her—the tender passion, the joy and love and laughter—were gone. She had killed it. And this was crazy; no good could come out of it; she had to stop...

'You're hurting me.' He wasn't and they both knew it.

'Hurting you? I couldn't hurt you if I tried; you proved that two years ago.' He raised his head to look down into the green-gold eyes staring up at him, the pupils big and dilated. 'And I told you before, physical force is not my style. But then, we both know you are enjoying this as much as me, don't we?' His fingers casually brushed the soft swell of her breasts, her nipples taut and hard under the cotton top she was wearing, and she knew her body was giving the 'go' signal in a manner as old as time.

'I can't touch your heart—if you have one,' he added cynically. 'But I can find out if taking you now will get rid of the annoying physical desire I have for your body.'

He made it sound as unimportant as if he were trying out a new remedy for an irritating attack of influenza, and as his mouth sought hers again, impatiently now, she began to fight him with all her might, twisting and turning in earnest as the hurt and pain and humiliation cut deep. She couldn't give in—*must not*.

'I don't want this, Hudson,' she panted desperately as she tried to roll from under the powerfully muscled frame holding hers so securely. 'I want you to stop. Do you hear me?'

'Why?' There was desire in his face—she could read that all too clearly in the dark red colour flaring across the high cheekbones and the naked hunger in his eyes—but the softness, the gentleness, the *caring* that had characterised his dealings with her in the past was totally absent. 'And why should it concern me what you want anyway?' he added cruelly. 'I haven't exactly noticed tears of regret and remorse for your conduct in the past.'

If only he knew—oh, if only he knew how much she had cried...

'If you behave like a cheap tease, or worse, then you should expect to be treated like one; isn't that the way it goes?' he suggested with chilling softness. 'I want you, Annie, and you want me—your body is telling me that, whatever your mouth says to the contrary. I've waited two years; I'm not prepared to wait a moment longer. And, however many others there've been, you'll remember this time.'

'I haven't slept around; you're making a mistake,' she gabbled frantically as he made to lower his head again. She dared not let him kiss her again because she knew, to her shame, that she wouldn't be able to resist him if he began to make love to her a second time.

Her breasts were still tight and heavy and begging for his touch, and the dull, sweet ache at the core of her that had grown into a wild, hot pain was almost too powerful to resist. She was fighting herself as much as him— more, maybe—and it was that which was frightening her to death. If she was joined to him, in body as well as heart, she wouldn't be able to let him walk away without telling him the truth; she knew it. She wouldn't be able to bear it.

'I don't believe you.' His eyes were on her lips, their dark grey depths glittering and sensuous. 'You're lying, sweet Annie.'

'No, I'm not.' She was crying now, tears of pain and desire and love. 'There...there hasn't been anyone. I've never... I didn't sleep with...with him, with anyone—'

'You ran away with him, disappeared for months on end without a word to anyone, and you expect me to believe you weren't living together?' he asked incredulously. 'What the hell do you take me for?' But he had raised himself slightly, the menacingly male body no longer touching her softness.

'That's how it was.' She had to think quickly, provide some reason—some excuse—that would let him still believe she had left him for someone else but that she wasn't available for a light affair with every Tom, Dick or Harry, as he seemed to assume.

'And Keith?' he asked grimly. 'What about him?'

'I told you, we're just friends.' She tried to dry her tears with her fingertips, her hands trembling. 'It's the truth, Hudson.'

'Annie, you wouldn't know the truth if it stood up and bit you.' His eyes narrowed still further, becoming grey pinpoints of steel in the darkness of his face. 'There's something wrong here, something not right; I can feel it,' he said grimly. 'I don't know what it is, but I do know you can't fool me any more; that time is past. But...there's no reason for you to lie about your virginity—if you *are* saying you're a virgin?' he asked slowly.

She nodded quickly, her face flaming with humiliation. 'I am.'

'Curiouser and curiouser, as Lewis Carroll would have said.' She could see the astute, formidable mind ticking over as he absorbed this new information. She kept absolutely still, knowing that the desire that was still hot and fierce between them needed only a slight fanning of the banked-down flames to flare into a raging inferno that would consume them both. 'Right—explain.' He rolled away suddenly, sitting up with his back against the trunk of a tree as he surveyed her with cool, dark eyes.

'Explain?' It was the one thing she couldn't do, and she stared at him for a second before struggling into a sitting position herself, knowing the tears wouldn't exactly have enhanced her already bedraggled appearance. She must look such a sight!

'Here.' He flung a crisp white handkerchief into her lap, but stayed where he was, his gaze intent. 'And don't even think of lying,' he warned softly, his voice even and controlled. 'Because rest assured I shall know. I listen to people perjuring themselves too often to mistake it.'

'I... I can't really explain. I can't, Hudson. It's over now, we've both got different lives; can't we just leave it at that and...and...?'

'And what?' he asked grimly as her gaze faltered beneath the stony eyes along with her stumbling voice. 'What do you suggest we do?'

'And part as friends?' she asked hopefully, her voice shaking.

'Annie, that is the most absurd thing you are ever likely to say.' He shook his head slowly, his mouth taut. 'Quite the most absurd.'

'I don't see why,' she said quickly. 'You liked me once—'

'I didn't *like* you,' he countered softly. 'I loved you, Annie, and this is something quite different. Love and hate are first cousins, did you know that? Perhaps not, but through loving you I learnt what hate is too—and believe me when I say you are not my friend. I want an explanation, Annie, and I want it fast.'

'I...I know.' She longed to tell him the truth, to put the burden of the decision on him, to let him take the pain and disappointment and bitterness and share it with her, but she couldn't. His career was his life—he had once told her that the only thing he had ever wanted to be was a lawyer, that he couldn't have imagined being anything else, and, knowing Hudson as she did, she knew, whatever he did, he would have to be the best at it.

Oh, she wished Michael Caxton had never been born...

'Michael told you there was someone else—'

'Are you going back to your original line that that is untrue?' he interrupted caustically, his face darkening.

'No, not exactly,' she said carefully, keeping her eyes fixed on his with superhuman control. His face was a little thinner, leaner, than two years ago, although he had been superbly fit then, and the slight weight loss made him look even more dangerous, sexier... 'It's just that I had no intention of settling down with anyone else when I left you,' she said quietly, the ring of honesty in her voice unmistakable to his trained ears. 'It wasn't like that. I wanted... I *needed* to cut all the ties from the past and make a new life for myself, concentrate... concentrate on my career.'

'Are you telling me you ran out on this other guy too?' Hudson asked flatly. 'That you dumped both of us?'

'I'm telling you I went to London by myself,' she said firmly. 'I wanted to make my own way, without any emotional commitments—'

'Without me, you mean.' He stared at her, the grey eyes that were so piercingly intuitive tight on her pale face. 'Now, why do I believe the first part and not the second?' he said thoughtfully, almost to himself. 'Why did you leave him behind, Annie? Wouldn't he play ball and follow you like an obedient little dog, or did he dump you when he found out about me? Is that why you cut off all contact with your family? Did they spill the beans about your sordid little fling in France and it made you angry with them?'

'If you want to believe that, believe it.' She could feel herself struggling in the sticky spider's web her lies had woven—she wasn't used to lying, and this was proving she wasn't any good at it either. She couldn't think quickly enough.

'So you didn't marry him, you didn't play house, and there's no one else on the scene at the moment? And, if I read you right, you're saying you deliberately keep it that way? Yes?'

'Yes.' She licked dry lips and his eyes followed the action.

'Why?' he asked grimly, his gaze still on her mouth.

'Why?' she repeated vacantly, her mind spinning.

'You are a beautiful young woman of twenty-five living by yourself in a city full of young men. You are intelligent, witty, and you have proved you can get a good job and keep it. Why are you content to act like an old-age pensioner with a houseful of animals to replace any social life? You haven't got a houseful of cats and dogs, have you?' he asked suddenly.

'No, I haven't.' She felt a spurt of angry adrenalin flood her system at the sad picture he was painting of her.

'Then I come back to my original question—why?' he repeated with silky persistence. 'You enjoyed our lovemaking as far as it went; I know that, Annie. And you were there with me today every inch of the way until you got cold feet. If it's like you said, if you got rid of this other guy too, what stops you making any sort of emotional commitment to a man? Have you been hurt? Abused, perhaps? Is that it? Did he abuse you sexually? Or someone else in your past? A friend of your mother's, perhaps?' he asked softly.

'No!' She was mortified at the way his mind was going.

'Don't look so embarrassed,' he said mildly. 'I deal with such things every day in my work—'

'I told you, I haven't... I haven't slept with anyone,' she interrupted wildly, her face fiery.

'You don't have to have done to have been hurt in some way.' It was a statement, not a question, and as he spoke he rose to his feet and walked over to her, drawing her up by her hands.

'You're trembling,' he murmured softly, drawing her against the hard wall of his chest as his hands began stroking her slender back, his touch slow and sensuous. 'Do I frighten you that much?'

If it had been fear that held her in its grip she could have coped, she thought helplessly. But it wasn't fear that was sending tiny little shivers flickering down every nerve and sinew and making her breathing shallow. He was wearing an expensively delicious aftershave, but beneath it was the scent of clean male skin, and pressed as she was into his shirt-front she could feel the primitive roughness of thick body hair beneath the silk, and it was driving what lucid thought remained clear away. He was so big, so male.

'I don't like secrets, Annie.' She couldn't see his face, folded as she was against his body, but his voice was flat and controlled. 'Put it down to the lawyer in me, or just that I'm an inquisitive so-and-so who doesn't know when to accept defeat, but I've never been able to let go until I've got to the bottom of anything I don't understand. And I don't understand this—or you. It would be simpler all round if you just spilled the beans now.'

'I...I can't.' She kept her face hidden. 'I can't.'

'No—you *won't*,' he corrected her evenly. 'You won't win if you fight me—no one does,' he warned softly. 'You must realise that?'

'I don't want to fight you.' She took a deep breath and prayed for strength to appear composed and calm. 'I told you, I just want to put the past behind us and part as friends. We have separate lives now. You're happy. I'm...I'm happy.'

'And I told you, you are the last person on this earth I would consider a friend,' he said expressionlessly.

It hurt, crucifyingly, causing her to jerk away so suddenly he was surprised into letting her go, and she kept her eyes lowered as she took a step backwards away from him and said, 'I...I have been hurt in the past— threatened, manipulated—but I can't discuss it with you or anyone else. Please, can't we just leave it at that?'

'Was it this man you went back to when you left me?' he asked softly, standing absolutely still as he spoke.

'No.' It was the rat who told you I'd got someone else, who was part of an organisation that would take fiendish delight in breaking you and watching you crawl or worse, who was married to my mother—*my mother*... 'That's all I'm saying, Hudson.' She raised drowning eyes to his, her misery so visible it stopped his breath.

'Except that I'm sorry I hurt you and…and let you down. I didn't mean to, but I realised I couldn't marry you, that it was impossible—with you or anyone else. I…I was stupid to let you think otherwise.'

Impossible with you because it would destroy you— impossible with anyone else because I couldn't bear to let another man touch me, loving you as I do, she thought numbly.

'And that's it? That's as much as you are going to say?' he asked slowly after a long moment when his eyes searched each feature of her white face. 'You expect me to accept that and ask no more?'

If she tried to speak again she would break down completely—in an effort to keep control, she was already biting her lip so hard she could taste blood, and so she merely nodded, a short, sharp little bob of her head, which, along with her clenched hands and deathly pale face, spoke volumes to the big man who had spent most of his working life calculating just how far he could push another human being before they reached breaking point.

'Okay.' It was cool and calm and casual, and totally at odds with all that had gone on before.

'Okay?' she asked weakly, her mind refusing to accept his capitulation. 'What do you mean, ''okay''?'

'Okay, fine, no problem…' He smiled, and she was too nervous and keyed up—her nerves stretched tight and rigid—to notice that the narrowed grey eyes were as cold and dark as deep water, and just as fathomless.

CHAPTER FOUR

MARIANNE hadn't expected to enjoy any part of the afternoon, but amazingly, once they had left the car and begun to wander around the massive enclosure the market was held in, she found the alien sights and smells too fascinating to resist.

The area was very busy—Hudson had told her on the way there that the weekly meeting place was as much a social occasion for visiting friends and catching up on the news, as the buying and selling of wares—and very colourful. It was clear the day was one which loomed large in the lives of the countrypeople, taking the place of cinemas, church fairs, and other entertainment the western world enjoyed as its right.

'A taste of the real Morocco.' Hudson's voice was soft and appreciative and mirrored her thoughts exactly, but then, as he took her hand, his flesh warm and firm, all her senses were tied up with the big male figure at her side.

They could have been an ordinary couple on holiday doing a bit of sightseeing, she thought with a touch of hysteria, and probably appeared so to anyone observing them. If nothing else, the last two years had taught her never to assume that what she could see and hear was necessarily as it seemed—that to accept people or situations at face value was a grave mistake. Some people spent their whole lives putting on a brave front—she understood that now in a way she could never have done before she had met Hudson, and before Michael had destroyed their happiness so cruelly.

'Home-made soap.' Hudson pointed to a large basket behind which a darkly bearded Moroccan man sat, his brown skin like leather. 'He'll have cooked it up by boiling ashes from his kitchen fire with fat cut from meat. The old ways still flourish here once you're out of the big towns and cities.'

'I see.' He seemed to be doing a roaring trade, Marianne thought as she smiled into the bright beady eyes watching them, receiving a gap-toothed grin in return.

One farmer had several clusters of live chickens with their feet tied together and their heads hanging down. Another had vegetable produce, another baskets of eggs. At one spot a great pile of yellow melons stood, and next to them a wizened little old Arab was crouching beside a small charcoal fire burning in a brazier. He was cooking sizzling chunks of mutton on skewers and selling them to the waiting crowd, who then moved on to the water-carrier nearby, who was exchanging a cupful of water from his goatskin for a few small coins. Marianne was fascinated by the almost biblical scene.

It was vibrant and colourful, and so different from life in the city that Marianne had the strange feeling she had stepped back in time, that she had been transported to another age, another world.

Would that she had been… She glanced at Hudson from under her eyelashes as the thought took form. A world where no Michaels had ever existed—no past, no future, just…now. Here with Hudson, touching him, feeling him close, she could almost imagine it…almost. She looked away, her heart thudding. Careful, Marianne, careful, she told herself tightly. She had to be cautious, always keep her guard up and perpetuate the subterfuge that was as abhorrent as it was necessary. He was too intelligent for less.

'Have you thought of me once or twice over the last two years, Annie?'

It was said without any recognisable emotion or expression, and took a moment or two to sink in, but then her eyes shot to his face and she saw he was looking at her with that intent grey gaze that betrayed very little. 'Have you?' he repeated calmly.

'I... Y-yes, of course,' she stammered weakly. 'Sometimes.'

'Sometimes.' He nodded thoughtfully. 'And what coloured those thoughts? Any touch of regret or remorse?'

'I...' He was still holding her hand, and must have felt the convulsive jerk of her fingers, but the cool, relaxed face was quite unreadable, his eyes shuttered and remote. 'Hudson...' Her voice trailed away again as she felt panic rip through her, even as she told herself she had to speak, to act normally, to play the part she had chosen—no, the part that had been *forced* on her, she corrected silently—as best she could. He was too intuitive, too perceptive for her to stammer and stutter her way through. 'There's no point in this conversation.'

'You're such a mix of personalities under that smooth, silky skin, aren't you?' he observed with a flatness that was unnerving. 'You make me feel like one of those game-show hosts—"Will the real Marianne Harding please stand up?"—you know?' He smiled, but it held no humour at all. 'But you wouldn't, would you?' he added slowly. 'I see that now.'

'Wouldn't what?' she asked bewilderedly.

'Let me see the real you.' His eyes were keen on her flushed face and she stared at him, searching her mind for a reply that just wouldn't materialise for some moments.

'You make me sound quite mysterious,' she managed at last.

But he turned as she spoke, gesturing to a big basket of sun-ripened cherries an elderly farmer was trying to sell as he asked, in fluent French, how much the fruit was.

They ate the succulent red cherries sitting on an old stone wall overlooking the market-place, the afternoon sun hot but without the fierceness of midday, and the venerable stones warm and mellow. It was a tranquil spot, a soft agelessness to the scene that was terribly poignant.

Marianne knew she would remember the interlude all her life—the bright sunshine, the smells and sights, the feel of the ancient warm stone under her legs and the taste of the cherries on her tongue. And Hudson. Hudson...

'Are you happy, Annie? With your exciting London life and wonderful job?' he asked softly, when she least expected it. 'Does your career give you everything you need?'

No, it didn't even begin to. 'Very much so,' she said brightly, his words making her finish her last cherry in one gulp, stone and all. 'Does yours?' she asked with a brittle smile.

'My career?' He shook his head slowly. 'It's a big part of my life but it doesn't consume me. I have other...pleasures.'

I know, I've seen one of them at the hotel, she thought fiercely as a dart of pain so sharp as to be unbearable shot through her chest. 'That's nice.' She forced another smile.

'Isn't it?' he agreed drily, his gaze moving from her face to the bustling scene in front of them, most of the traders beginning to pack their wares and purchases for the long trek home by donkey, bus or bicycle, few of them being able to afford their own car. 'I like to think I'm well-rounded. The old adage of all work and no play still holds good in this frantic age. I've seen more men collapse with overwork than anything else. There has to be a balance in life...enjoyment.'

She had no doubt at all that the luscious redhead could give him all the enjoyment he could handle, Marianne thought tightly. 'Quite.' She tried to make her voice even but it came out more as a snap, and to cover up she said quickly, 'Do...do you play a sport? Something you do to relax?'

She didn't believe she'd just said that. As the

smoky-grey gaze turned her way she wanted to curl up and die at the dark amusement in his eyes. How could she have put it like that?

'Don't you remember?' he asked softly. 'Two years isn't that long.'

'I... No— At least, I don't think...'

'Squash.' The grey eyes were relishing her hot-faced, mumbling confusion. 'I play squash, Annie,' he said mockingly.

'Right.' She nodded like a demented parrot. 'Squash. Yes.'

'Among other things.'

They arrived back at the car with the late-afternoon sun still high in the sky, and as Marianne slid inside the suffocatingly hot interior she took her hat off and tossed it onto the back seat, looping all the hair she could gather back into the knot on top of her head to cool her over-heated neck. The car was like a sauna.

'It's still like spun gold and as fine as silk.'

'What?' As Hudson joined her in the car his voice was deep and throaty, but so velvety-soft she thought she had misheard him.

'Your hair.' His eyes sent trickles of sensation shivering down her spine as they wandered over her, their darkness mesmerising. 'I've known other women who have tried to achieve that sort of look but never quite pulled it off, but with you it's natural, isn't it?' He shook his head slowly. 'And lethal,' he added darkly.

'What sort of look?' she asked warily. There was something in his voice—just the merest something—that made her wonder if he was being complimentary or insulting.

'Temptation with restraint, a sort of come-hither appeal but with the proviso that the unfortunate male doesn't come *too* close,' he said thoughtfully. 'Sex and innocence—it's a deadly combination and you do it very well.'

'I'm not trying to tempt anybody,' she objected heatedly, warm colour staining her cheeks at his description of a teasing *femme fatale*. 'I wear my hair this way for me, that's all, and I like it long,' she added militantly, her eyes flashing green sparks.

'Oh, so do I, and probably the rest of the male population would say the same,' he murmured drily.

'That's not my problem.' She glared at him—hurt beyond measure at the suggestion she was trying to entice unfortunate men to their doom, like the sirens of Greek mythology. 'Anyway, should you really be here now with me?' she asked tightly. 'Surely the current lady, whoever she is, might object?'

'Why should she?' In direct contrast to her crumbling control, his manner was one of cool self-possession and calm, his voice serene, aloof even. 'We mean nothing to each other now; you know it and I know it. This is just an…interlude, a catching up on old times, if you like,' he said smoothly.

She didn't like. She didn't like at all. And the fact that she was hurt, angry—whatever the name was for the sensation of raging pain in the pit of her stomach—at his apparent ability to turn his emotions on and off like a tap was doubly worrying. She wanted him to want her as he had earlier that afternoon, to desire her body if nothing else, and now apparently even that weakness was under control.

But she shouldn't want him to want her. The thought darkened her eyes to black emerald, causing the light gold flecks to stand out in sharp contrast. She should be glad he was over her, that he'd made a life without her, with…with someone else. She *should*. She found she wasn't cut out to be a martyr as jealousy cut deep.

He stared at her intently for a second, his face imperturbable and his thoughts hidden from her, before turning and starting the engine, his movements controlled and collected.

'We'd better get you back to the hotel,' he said quietly. 'It wouldn't do for the reputable Keith to imagine you were actually enjoying being in my company, would it? He might get the wrong idea.' He glanced at her, his eyes mocking now.

'I thought that was the point of this game you're playing,' Marianne said tightly, fighting back the tears that were gathering like hot acid at the back of her eyes, and willing her voice not to falter.

'Is that what you think this is? A game?' he asked flatly, harshness twisting his lips and turning the hard planes of his face to chiselled stone. 'This is no game, Annie. I grew out of games a long, long time ago. No, whatever this is—and you'll find out soon enough—it's deadly serious. In my line of work...' He paused for a moment, his eyes hard on her white face before he continued, 'In my line of work retribution isn't always forthcoming, more's the pity, but where it's in my power to redress the balance I do so. I find it...satisfying, I have to admit.'

'And that's how you see this?' she asked faintly. 'Us?'

'There is no "us", you made that perfectly clear two years ago,' he said coolly, his gaze piercingly intent. 'Didn't you?'

'Yes, but—'

'There can be no "buts", Annie, not in a situation like this. A broken appointment, a momentary hiccup in communication, that could qualify as a "but". But the severance of two hearts? I think not.' His eyes were burning into her mind, their glittering depths searching and concentrated. 'You walked away from me and you left a piece of paper to explain why. And it didn't.'

'What do you want from me?' she whispered tremblingly. His capitulation earlier that day had been too easy; she might have known.

His hard, sensuous mouth took hers and she was too surprised at first to resist, but the kiss only lasted a few seconds, its bruising fierceness hungry and wild. And then the control was there again, governing his moving away from her shaking body and fully into his own seat as he allowed the growling engine to have its head and spring the car forward.

'All in good time,' he said coolly. 'All in good time.'

'If you think I'm going to put up with this then you're very much mistaken. I'm not some mindless bimbo you can order about.'

She had wanted to sound outraged, strong and firm, but even to her own ears her voice was weak and trembling.

'With what?' he asked evenly, sparing her one sardonic glance before concentrating on the road again. 'An afternoon out? A relaxed picnic with an old... acquaintance? A few hours' sightseeing? What is so terrible about that, Annie? You're going to be delivered back to the hotel in time for dinner and before your evening's work, aren't you? Exactly as I promised.'

If he thought she was going to have dinner with him, he could think again. She glared at the cool profile, her cheeks fiery and her heart sore. And she would tell him so, in no uncertain terms, when they got back to the hotel. He was an arrogant brute...

As it happened there was no need. After parking the car, Hudson took her arm as they walked across to the hotel, and, just as she had perfected the bitingly composed refusal she had been practising all the way back, she saw a group of people who looked vaguely familiar waiting in Reception.

'Hudson...' As a low, throaty voice spoke his name at the same time as the redhead—who had been obscured by a tall, portly man—moved into view, Marianne realised where she had seen them before. 'We've been waiting for you for ages, sweetie; the show starts at seven, remember?' the redhead drawled huskily as she took his arm.

'I haven't forgotten.' Hudson nodded at them all before turning to glance down at Marianne, his eyes remote. 'Goodbye, Annie. Enjoy your evening,' he said coolly.

Marianne was conscious of making some reply, although she couldn't have told anyone exactly what, before she carried on past the group and over to the lift, almost falling into the interior of the carpeted box and having to force herself to turn round and face Reception as she pressed the button for her floor. They had gone—Reception was empty.

That would teach her! The thought was hot and caustic, and continued to hammer its way home all through dinner—of which she barely ate a bite—and the evening shoot which followed, so that by the time she arrived back at the hotel that night her head was thudding with a sick headache and her neck was as stiff as a board. She took two aspirins, showered and went to bed.

She slept badly and awoke tired and dull-eyed, joining the others at breakfast in something of a dream, and then snapping fully awake as she glanced across the dining room and saw Hudson sitting in solitary contentment, enjoying what looked like a huge breakfast. She hated him. She did; she loathed him! He had no right to look so at ease and cool and *satisfied* when she was falling apart inside. How dared he eat such a huge breakfast?

As though her thoughts had communicated themselves across the room, he raised his head as she watched him, meeting her eyes with a distant coldness and nodding dismissively before continuing with his meal. As a snub it was a prize-winner.

That incident set the tone for the next three days until the job was finished, and reduced Marianne to a quivering, nervous wreck. If she happened to see Hudson about the hotel at any time, he was courteous and polite and terribly remote, exchanging the barest of niceties before going his own way.

Marianne worked all day and cried most of the nights, and by her last evening at the hotel—Keith and the others having left Tangier that afternoon as soon as the shoot was finished—she felt like a limp rag, and would have given the world just to go home to England and her little flat rather than embark on the proposed trip round Morocco's cities. But something deep inside, a feeling compounded of pride, self-preservation and a strange kind of fortitude that wouldn't let her creep away and hide, kept her to her original plan.

And it was this same feeling that drove her downstairs to the dining room that evening, rather than ordering a meal to be sent up to her room, although she knew Hudson would probably be eating there—if he wasn't already out with the redhead.

It had become apparent over the last few days that his girlfriend wasn't staying at the hotel, but the tall, voluptuous female figure had cropped up with monotonous regularity in the evenings—Hudson either dining with her and his other friends at the hotel, or a crowd of them going elsewhere to eat after meeting in Reception. And it had become increasingly hard to take.

Idris and Fatima had been in the group once or twice, both of them waving and nodding to her on the occasion when—the night before—they had caught her eye, and, ridiculously, it had somehow seemed to make things worse.

So now, as Marianne left the lift and walked purposefully into the dining room, she carried her head high and held her back straight in spite of the trembling in the pit of her stomach that threatened to communicate itself to her legs. He could have a whole bevy of females dancing attendance for all she cared, she told herself viciously. It was nothing to her. *He* was nothing to her.

'Hi there.'

She had just been seated at a secluded table for two in a discreet, quiet corner of the dining room by her favourite waiter, after explaining that the rest of her party had left earlier, when Hudson's deep, husky voice caused her eyes to freeze on the menu before she nerved herself to raise her head.

'Hello.' She was eternally grateful that he was alone—the way she had been feeling all day, she might well have burst into tears if his girlfriend had been with him, which would have been the ultimate humiliation. She even managed a fairly normal smile to match her cool voice.

'Are you dining alone?' he asked softly.

Her heart had given the most incredible lurch as her eyes had registered the dark, latent power in the big, immaculately clothed male body and powerfully hand-some face, and now all she could do was nod weakly in answer to his enquiry, not trusting her voice.

'Then do you mind if I join you?' he asked with easy confidence.

'I... That is...'

'Why don't I just sit down while you make up your mind?'

It was the cool arrogance that put steel in her back-bone, and she found herself saying, in tones that could only be described as tart, 'Because I might not want you to.'

'Too late.' He smiled, but the glittering gaze was in-tent on her face. 'I'm seated now, and it really wouldn't do to cause a scene on your last night, would it?' he suggested mockingly.

'I don't care.' And at that moment she didn't; she really didn't.

'Ah, fighting talk.' He leant back in the chair, stretch-ing slightly as he surveyed her with narrowed eyes, be-fore saying, 'Then take pity on the other diners if noth-ing else. They are just out to have a pleasant meal in comfortable surroundings. Don't deprive them of what is—after all—just a passing pleasure.' He looked very satisfied with himself and it rankled unbearably.

'And you are an authority on passing pleasures.' The moment the words had left her lips she could have

kicked herself. The last thing—*the very last thing*—she
wanted him to think was that she was bothered, in any
way, by his relationship with the redhead; the probability
that he would assume she was jealous was not to be
borne. She had to think before she spoke!

'Retract those claws, pussycat,' he murmured drily.
'I'm suggesting we share a table for dinner, that's all.'

The appearance of a smiling wine waiter, who was all
white teeth and slicked-down black hair, stopped the angry retort she was about to hiss at Hudson, which was
probably just as well, she reflected wryly as Hudson ordered a superior bottle of wine from the wine menu. This
situation needed coolness, composure and calm control.
But knowing it and doing it were two vastly different
things.

'And where is the gentle, good-natured Keith?' Hudson drawled lazily, parodying her earlier description of
Keith with a cruel smile, once the wine waiter had departed with an attentive bow.

She glared at him, biting back the furious retort hovering on her tongue with extreme difficulty. She didn't
want to reveal that the others had already left Tangier
because that would involve an explanation as to why she
had stayed on, and suddenly the fact that she was taking
a holiday alone was...embarrassing. She could have
asked any one of a number of friends to accompany
her—in fact several had suggested it when they had
heard of her plans—but she hadn't wanted company.
However, Hudson might assume she was alone through
necessity—not choice—and the image of a tall, slim female with flaming red hair made that possibility unbearable.

She shrugged carefully, forcing herself to think before
she spoke. 'Keith? Why should I know where he is? I
told you before, I work for him, that's all. He certainly
doesn't have to answer to me for his whereabouts.'

'I don't see any of the others around either.' He
moved casually in his chair, glancing round the dining

room with narrowed eyes before turning back to her. 'Are they joining you later?'

'No.' She tried, very hard, for a languid nonchalance as she said, 'I was looking forward to eating alone for once, as it happens,' with a pointed lift of her fine eyebrows.

'Oh, you do know where Keith is, then?' he asked easily.

'Hudson, I don't *care* where Keith is.' There, she had gone and bitten back when she had wanted to do just the opposite, she thought tightly. But as always his casual coolness had hit her on the raw. He was so—so *irritating*.

'Charming,' he drawled softly with infuriating censure. 'Is that really the way a devoted employee should refer to her boss? Especially when he's brought you to such a beautiful part of the world. Some would consider it the height of ingratitude.'

'I happen to be working,' Marianne snapped angrily. 'This is not a holiday, in case you hadn't noticed.'

'Of course it isn't,' he murmured, his voice coolly patronising.

She took a long, deep, hard pull of air and counted to ten—and then another ten—before saying, in tones of honeyed sweetness, 'And your friends? They aren't around tonight?'

'Sadly, no.' He smiled lazily. 'So it's just you and me.'

The wine waiter reappeared at that moment, his wide smile bright and ingratiating, and by the time the ritual of tasting and approving had been completed another waiter was hovering for their order. The activity eased the atmosphere a little, but Marianne found her heart was still hammering against her breastbone when Hudson's glittering gaze stroked her flushed face some moments later, once they were alone.

'It must soon be time for you to return to England,' he said idly, his long fingers playing with the stem of his wine glass and his eyes fixed tightly on hers. 'I take it the job's nearly finished?'

'Yes.' She nodded, without elaborating, and said quickly, 'When do you leave for the States?'

'In a few days.' He eyed her impassively. 'I'm in no rush.'

'Oh.' Talk, say something, get the conversation away from departure dates, she told herself agitatedly. 'Back to masses of work, no doubt?' Oh, how banal; couldn't you do better than that, Marianne? she thought caustically. Riveting conversation it wasn't.

'No doubt.' He continued to survey her with intent dark grey eyes for one moment more before straightening in his seat, his expression suddenly clearing and his smile dangerously innocent. 'But tell me some more about your work, Annie,' he said gently. 'It's clearly something that absorbs you and that you're good at.'

She looked at him very hard, trying to appraise whether there was a hidden meaning to the apparent interest, but decided to accept his words at face value—it was safer. 'I love it,' she agreed quietly. 'My father— my *real* father—was a keen photographer, and he used to take me out at weekends with him when I was a child. Scotland is a photographer's dream. When...when I went down to London it was a case of being in the right place at the right time, and things just...happened,' she finished uncomfortably.

'How fortunate.' It was a slow drawl.

Again she wasn't sure if he was being nasty or not, but valiantly continued, 'Yes, it was. So many employers won't even grant an interview to someone without experience, but Keith was prepared to give me a chance.'

'After he'd seen you,' Hudson said expressionlessly. 'How kind.'

'Yes, and everything just...'

'Happened.' He nodded slowly. 'Well, that's really good, Annie. And you're happy and contented and the epitome of a thrusting nineties woman, yes? Fulfilled, strong, satisfied...'

She went brick-red but she couldn't help it. It was the way he had drawled the last word—as a subtle challenge but something else too, the word carrying a dark heat that connected in the pit of her stomach and caused a dull, sweet ache.

'More wine?' Hudson suggested lazily.

Too late she realised she had been sipping rather frantically at the mellow, fruity red wine and that her glass was empty. She watched, mesmerised, as he refilled the crystal with deep red liquid, and warned herself this glass would have to be her last. The deliciously expensive wine was potent and she needed all her wits.

Nevertheless, the alcohol provided welcome stimulation, enabling her to hold her own in the conversation over dinner without too many awkward pauses, and by the time coffee was served—some two hours later—she realised she had drunk more than she had intended.

What was he doing? Softening her up for the big seduction scene? she asked herself grimly as the waiter poured them both a tiny cup of the thick black aromatic coffee the Moroccans favoured. He knew her time in Tangier was drawing to a close. She was alone, he was alone... She might have guessed. That was it.

'Something is wrong, Annie?'

The piercing eyes were too intuitive and she struggled to clear her face and her voice as she said, with a touch too much brightness, 'Wrong? Of course not. Whatever could be wrong? That was a lovely meal—'

'Then perhaps it is the company.' It was said with a smile, his voice teasing and light, but she was still looking at his eyes, and they were cold, their greyness deep and chilling.

Marianne shivered suddenly, an icy awareness flickering over her skin as she realised that for the whole evening he had been playing a part—that of amusing, courteous dinner companion. *But he wasn't feeling like that inside.* All the clever talk, the light anecdotes with which he had kept her entertained were merely a smoke-screen for what was really going on in that ruthless, ra-pier-sharp brain of his. This was a courtroom situation to him—he would give nothing away and capitalise on any weakness without mercy. Her skin began to tingle and burn, and she felt weak, light-headed.

'No, it isn't the company,' she said quickly. 'It's just been a long day, that's all. The whole schedule has been a tight one. Perhaps I'm just tired.' She smiled nervously and he smiled back.

'Perhaps.' His voice was smooth and soft, like raw silk, and he glanced at the heavy gold watch on his wrist before saying, 'Still, you can have an early night, can't you? It isn't late.'

'Yes…' She wasn't at all sure where he was coming from but something was putting that glittering coldness in his eyes.

'Unless Keith has lined some work up for you to-night?'

'No—I mean…I don't think so. There's nothing ar-ranged—' Calm down; don't lose it now, she told herself tensely as she heard herself babbling, and stopped abruptly. 'I think everyone will have an early night to-night,' she finished lamely. 'We're all tired.'

'I'm sure they will.' The chill deepened. 'In fact Keith and the others should just be landing by now, shouldn't they?'

He had known. All the time he had known!

'What did you think I was going to do if I knew you were alone?' he asked. 'Force my way into your room and take you by force? Or pester you? Make life un-pleasant?'

'I didn't think that; of course I didn't,' Marianne said defensively, her face flaming with embarrassment.

'No? Forgive me if I say I don't believe you.' He looked at her steadily, some deep emotion at the back of his eyes that she couldn't fathom. Anger? Bitterness? Hurt pride?

'Hudson, it wasn't like that—' Marianne protested, before he cut in in his usual sweeping manner, his voice arrogant and proud.

'I'm not really interested one way or the other, Annie, so save your breath. Now, I'm sure you're tired, and I've things to do...'

'Hudson—'

'Goodnight, Annie, sleep well.' It was very frosty and very final.

And then he had gone, rising in one swift, fluid movement and walking out of the dining room without a backward glance, his broad shoulders straight and firm and his head held high.

Damn. Damn, damn, damn... She stared after him for long moments, her eyes jade-green with pain. She hadn't wanted it to end like this; she hadn't. Their last exchange would be one of bitterness and misunderstanding; he would hate her still more when he found her gone in the morning. Should she follow him? Explain about her trip? Say goodbye properly? She half rose in her seat.

Properly? That deep inner voice mocked her, its sudden intrusion into the maelstrom of panic caustic and unwelcome. What was 'properly'? To weep all over him? To persuade him to feel sorry for her? To beg his forgiveness? To tell him the one thing she couldn't say? Was that what she wanted? Where was her backbone?

She had set her feet on the path she had to follow two years ago and there was no turning back now, however much her heart craved otherwise. If she loved him, *really* loved him—and she did, oh, she did—she had to let him go. Anything else was self-indulgent and cruel. It was better for him to think she was heartless, to wash his hands of her once and for all.

Marianne walked to her room on leaden feet, glancing over her shoulder once more before she opened the door and walked in annoyed at finding herself hoping... Hoping what? she asked herself with furious self-contempt. That he would be standing waiting for her? That he would have followed her because he couldn't bear to leave her on such terms? Fool, fool, fool. Even if her hopes had come true it would have spelt disaster for them both. And, anyway, she knew Hudson was a fiercely proud and cynical man, and such men didn't abase themselves for someone who had already jilted them once.

It was over. It had been dealt a death-blow two years ago and the death-throes were finally finished.

CHAPTER FIVE

THE night was endless. Marianne sat in a small basket chair on her balcony after showering and changing into her nightie and towelling robe, the warmth of the sultry night pleasant without being sticky. The moon was shedding a thin, hollow light over the face of the ocean far down in the bay, and one by one lights were dimmed and extinguished as people slept.

She had allowed him to touch the quintessence of her mind... She rubbed a tired hand over her face as she acknowledged the truth of the thought. He had got deep inside her head again, taken over every little part of her, but then...perhaps he had always been there. She had been fooling herself all these long, lonely months when she had been telling herself time was a great healer, that she was getting over him.

Getting over him. The phrase mocked her. You didn't get over Hudson de Sance. She might learn to live with the pain, go on and exist—function—the way people the world over did when catastrophe hit them, but with his departure from her life something essentially joyful and beautiful had died in her spirit. Whatever she did in the future, wherever she went, she would carry him with her in her heart. A bleak desolation filled her senses.

Dawn crept across the sky in a soft explosion of pink and cinnamon, touching the last remaining shadows with colour and making her cry with its beauty, and still she hadn't slept.

At six she rose slowly from her seat, like an old woman, and made her way to the bathroom, standing for long, long minutes under the warm shower and letting the smooth, silky water drown her tears and wash her clean. Life had to go on; *she* had to go on.

She dried her mass of golden hair sitting back in the basket chair as she watched the sun rise in a cloudless blue sky that promised a hot day, and later, after dressing simply in a loose white shirt and matching skirt, didn't bother to put it up, leaving it in a cloud of tiny curls about her neck and shoulders. She didn't bother with any make-up either; she just didn't have the energy, and since coming to Morocco the sun had tinted her smooth skin with its own honey shade which make-up couldn't enhance.

The coach was picking her up early outside Reception and she had decided to have her breakfast as soon as the dining room was open, before most of the other residents would be awake. Consequently, she wasn't surprised that the huge, sun-splashed room was virtually empty, with just the odd tourist who had a plane or coach to catch dotted around its vast space.

She had just helped herself to a croissant, still warm from the oven, and a bowl of freshly prepared papaw from the magnificent buffet, and was turning to find a quiet table for one in a secluded corner, when a deep voice in her ear caused her to start so violently, most of the papaw jumped onto the floor.

'Early bird.' Hudson's voice was like warm treacle and devoid of any trace of the emotion of the night before.

'Hudson!' She took a step backwards from the papaw, which a helpful waiter was already rushing to clear up, straight onto Hudson's foot, and promptly dropped the whole bowl. 'Oh, now look what you've made me do,' she said fretfully, overwhelmingly glad the dining room was virtually deserted.

'I beg your forgiveness.' His voice was dry now, and as she turned to face him properly she felt her heart jerk and thud and then race on at a furious rate. He was dressed in casual wide-cut cotton trousers in a pale shade

of grey which sat on the lean hips in a way guaranteed
to make any female take a second glance, and his silky
charcoal shirt accentuated the brooding masculinity to
perfection. He looked cool and controlled and dangerous—very, very dangerous, Marianne thought breathlessly. And gorgeous. *Definitely* gorgeous.

'You're…you're up early.' It was pathetic, but all she
could do with her heart hammering so hard it hurt and
her face as red as a beetroot. She had thought she
wouldn't see him again…

'So are you.' He smiled, gesturing across the room to
a small table for two. 'Go and sit down and I'll get you
another bowl of fruit—papaw, was it?' he said as he
eyed the mess on the floor.

'Yes, please, but you needn't… I mean, I can manage—'

'Go and sit down, Annie,' he said patiently, his all-
encompassing glance at her flushed face taking in her
confusion and embarrassment. 'You're making me nervous.'

She went and sat—it was easier than arguing with
him. Besides which the thought of a few more minutes
with him, before the inevitable goodbyes were said, was
too enticing to resist.

Of course, it wouldn't help the actual parting, once
breakfast was over, that he looked so good this morning,
Marianne thought dispiritedly as she watched the tall,
lean figure across the room. And perhaps last night, painful though it was, had been the best way for them to say
goodbye. If he was nice to her and she cried all over
him… Oh, she couldn't, she thought, horror-stricken. No
way.

Just before he came over to the table she saw one of
the girls from Reception enter the dining room and walk
over to him, exchanging a brief word before leaving
again. She didn't think anything of it until, after he had
seated himself, he said, 'The bellboy has fetched your
luggage down as arranged.'

'Has he?' She stared at him in surprise. Was that what the girl from Reception had just told him? she asked herself, puzzled. But why tell Hudson about her luggage?

'And it is now sitting comfortably in the back of my vehicle,' he added smoothly, reaching across to pour himself a cup of coffee as though it were a perfectly normal conversation.

'What?' She'd misheard him; she must have. 'What did you say?'

'Your luggage is in the back of my Range Rover.' He took a sip of the fragrant brew and sighed appreciatively. 'This is damn good coffee—'

'*Hudson?*' She tried not to shout—she really did—and failed.

'Yes?' The devastatingly intent gaze was raised to fix on her wide green eyes, and she saw it was as hard as iron.

'Did you just say—' she took a deep pull of air and tried to speak calmly '—that my luggage is in a vehicle belonging to you?'

'Well, if you're going to be precise about it, it's in a vehicle hired by me,' he said affably. 'I thought a Range Rover was far more suitable for long journeys out here—the roads are less than good in certain areas—but if you'd prefer a car...?'

'What I would *prefer*—' Again the deep gulp of air, but this time it didn't work and she could hear her voice rising shrilly as she continued, 'Is to know what on earth you're talking about. Why is my luggage in your Range Rover? Who told you to put it there? Because I certainly didn't. I'm leaving shortly—'

'I know.' Again the piercing eyes held hers. 'With me.'

'On a trip, if you must know,' she countered angrily, furious that he had extracted the information from her. 'It's a tour—'

'Taking in the five major cities of Morocco,' he finished calmly. 'Eat that papaw now I've brought it, Annie.'

'Blow the papaw.' She couldn't believe this; she really couldn't. Was he crazy or was it her? Because one of them definitely wasn't firing on all cylinders! 'Are you seriously telling me that you have taken it upon yourself to order that my luggage be given to you?' she hissed incredulously. 'Is that what you're saying?'

'Exactly.' He smiled, but it didn't reach the fathomless eyes as they moved consideringly over her flushed, angry face.

'Then un-order it now,' she commanded with scant regard for grammar. 'I've got a coach to catch this morning; it's due soon—'

'Wrong,' he said with smooth arrogance. 'Dead wrong.'

He was enjoying this, every minute of it, she thought angrily as she read the satisfaction he was making no effort to hide.

'Hudson, you'd better explain, *and fast*, before I empty this coffee jug over your head.' It wasn't an idle threat, and wiped the satisfaction away like magic, she noticed with some gratification.

'There is no coach,' he said hastily, reaching for the coffee jug and moving it to his side of the table. 'Marjorie cancelled it a few days ago, okay?'

'Marjorie?' What on earth had possessed Marjorie to cancel the coach? Marianne looked into Hudson's glittering eyes, and suddenly she knew.

'I was talking to Marjorie one evening a few nights ago,' Hudson continued easily, although she noticed he kept his hand on the coffee jug and his eyes didn't leave her furious face. 'She told me of your proposed trip, and as luck would have it I'd planned to do the same circuit myself.' One heavy eyebrow quirked at her but she ignored it.

'So...it seemed ridiculous—to Marjorie and myself—that you and I planned to do the trip separately, you in a hot bus and me in a great, spacious Range Rover. Follow so far?' he asked gently.

She glared at him and his hand tightened on the coffee jug.

'So Marjorie very kindly phoned on your behalf and cancelled your seat... They were very understanding,' he said approvingly.

'Where they?' she said grimly. 'And why didn't Marjorie tell me about this kindness? Or did it simply slip her memory?'

'We thought it would be better in the form of a surprise,' Hudson said coolly. 'Added to the fact that if I had asked you to travel round with me you would have said no. Marjorie...understands things like that.'

'Oh, does she? So the tour people were understanding, Marjorie was understanding, and clearly the bellboy was pretty understanding too. How much did you tip him to steal my luggage, Hudson? And what did you pay the others?'

'"Steal" is a nasty word, Annie,' he murmured reproachfully.

'It's a nasty act,' she shot back tightly. 'As well you know.'

'Don't be difficult, sweetheart.' The endearment was matter-of-fact but still hit her like a blow. 'I've explained the circumstances, and you will be far safer with me than alone with a crowd of strangers. This is all for the best.'

'I wouldn't exactly be alone with a crowd, now, would I?' she bit out testily. 'Besides which, that whole argument is crazy—'

'You're saying you wouldn't feel safe with me?' His tone was reproving but his eyes were wicked, and her fingers longed to take the bowl of papaw and throw it at him.

'What about your—?' She stopped abruptly. 'Your friend?' she continued tightly. 'I presume you've told her?'

'My friend?' His expression was innocently puzzled.

He knew; he knew exactly to whom she was referring! 'The...lady with the red hair,' she spelt out grimly, allowing the slightest pause that gave the word 'lady' unpleasant connotations. As if he didn't know.

'You mean Jasmine,' he supplied helpfully, his face earnest.

'Jasmine—right. Well, won't Jasmine object to our taking off into the great unknown together?' she asked stiffly, the name like acid on her lips. 'Won't she find it a bit...odd?'

'Why should she?' he enquired with infuriating innocence. 'She knows we are friends...old friends.'

'You said I could never be your friend.' She hadn't meant to say it, to betray the hurt it had caused, but somehow it just popped out, laced with all the pain she was feeling.

'There you are, then,' he said softly, his face shuttered and closed. 'We aren't even friends so there is nothing for her to worry about, is there? We will be merely fellow travellers, nothing more. Now, that croissant must be quite cold by now; would you like me to get you a warm one?' he asked evenly.

'No, I would not.' She couldn't believe she was in the middle of such a situation and that he was almost making her feel unreasonable by objecting to it. She had the maddening feeling she was allowing herself to be bullied, swept along by a will far stronger than hers and a mind that was certainly far more astute. And Marjorie... What on earth had he said to Marjorie to make her agree to enter into such a conspiracy? She knew the beautiful model was somewhat giddy, and thinking had never exactly been Marjorie's forte, but this! This was...well, it was...

'Eat up, then.' His grey eyes were intent on her face and he didn't smile as he spoke, watching her with a look that made her heart thud frantically again. He was so handsome—stunning, even—and she loved him so much. That in itself made any suggestion of three or four days alone with him too dangerous to consider.

'I intend to.' She forced a cool smile that was the best piece of acting she had ever done. 'And then you can take my luggage out of your Range Rover and I shall decide whether to fly home immediately or spend another few days here. Either way, there is no chance of us travelling together, so you might as well accept that now.' She eyed him firmly as the smile faded.

'No way,' he stated with soft determination. 'You're coming.'

'You're crazy—'

'Not at all.' He settled back in his seat as he spoke, his mouth smiling but his eyes cold. 'I am in complete control of my mind and my emotions and you know it. I want a companion to travel with and you are at hand; I see no problem with that.'

'Well, unfortunately for your wonderful plans, I do!' she bit back.

'You *will* travel with me, Annie.' He hadn't moved a muscle, but she felt as though he had reached out and gripped her mind as his eyes narrowed, pinpoints of glowing black fire deep in the depths of them. 'You want to see Morocco—so do I. It would be foolish to allow past history to interfere with what is only, after all, a brief interlude in our lives. We will be travelling together, exploring the sights, okay? You will be quite safe.' The last was said with heavy mockery, and immediately her hackles rose to meet it. 'I'll give you a written guarantee if you want.'

'I'm not frightened of you, Hudson,' she said tightly.

'Good. That's settled, then.' His tone was suddenly impatient. Clearly he considered there had been enough discussion on the subject and it was finished, and his next words confirmed this when he said, 'I presume you've already settled your account, and so have I. Now, I would suggest that you avail yourself of a cooked breakfast in addition to the fruit and croissant. I want to leave shortly, and I'm not sure when we will stop for lunch.'

She wasn't going to win this one. Not so much because Hudson had forced her into a corner—although that was bad enough—but because she wanted, *desperately*, to go with him. The thought was shocking but she acknowledged the truth of it.

She had thought, through all the long night hours when the rest of the world had been asleep and she had felt herself shrivel down into a little speck of empty nothingness, that she wouldn't see him again. And now he was offering her a few days of being with him, watching him, hearing him, before they had to part.

It was crazy—she was crazy—to agree to this incredible plan, but she was going to. She wasn't strong enough to fight both him and herself. But oh, she knew already she was going to regret it.

'Comfortable?'

'Yes, thank you,' Marianne replied with a certain stiffness that wasn't lost on the big man at her side as the Range Rover sped along the road in the gathering heat of the May morning.

'You're not going to sulk, are you?' Hudson asked softly. 'I appreciate you might have cause, but it's going to make the next few days wearisome for us both.' He smiled lazily.

'You appreciate I might have cause?' she asked in amazement. 'That's not what you said at the hotel.' She eyed him crossly.

'I still had to get you into the Range Rover then.' It was so like his brand of sweeping arrogance that she stared at him for a moment or two before she could formulate a reply that was coherent.

'Is that some kind of apology?' she asked shortly.

'Do you want it to be?' he murmured sardonically.

'I— You... Oh, I'm not discussing this any more,'

she finished hotly, snapping her gaze from him and staring angrily out of the windscreen. 'You're impossible.'

'Yes, it is an apology, Annie.' The vehicle slowed and then stopped, and he turned slightly in his seat to face her, his grey eyes narrowed and his firm mouth trying to hide the amusement she could read in the twist of his lips. 'Now, is that better?'

'You don't mean it, do you?' Marianne accused warily.

'Damn it all, woman, I can't win.' The tone was one of mocking reproach. 'If I don't apologise I'm in the wrong, and if I do you accuse me of lying. Isn't that right?'

'If you *meant* it—'

'I mean it, I mean it,' he interrupted, but there was a glint of laughter at the back of his eyes. 'Look, I'll apologise properly and try to convince you I'm suitably chastened.'

He had taken her lips before she realised his intention, his hands moving to either side of her head to hold her face still. The firm, sensuous mouth was demanding and she wanted to melt against him, to return the kiss, but she dared not, so she fought the desire—hard. She remained perfectly still with her eyes tightly shut, telling herself that if she allowed this now—if she responded now—the next few days would turn into... What? Paradise? Yes, very probably, but then the return to the real world at the end of it would be unbearable. And it *would* have to come.

'Stop fighting me.' It was a soft murmur against her lips and cut into the whirling confusion of her thoughts. 'You want me to kiss you—admit it. I know it and you know it.'

'I do not.' Now she did move, but it was to jerk away so violently that her head would have banged on the side window if it hadn't been open. 'You said this would be a trip of convenience, that's all, just keeping each other company,' she reminded him fiercely. 'Didn't you? And that means no lovemaking, Hudson.'

'Annie, I was only kissing you, for crying out loud—'

'*Didn't you?*' she insisted hotly. 'A platonic excursion?'

'That's what you want?' He looked at her steadily, his heavily lashed eyes searching her flushed face. 'What you *really* want?'

'Yes, that's what I want,' she said tremulously, the anger and fight dying at the look on his face.

'So be it.' And then, perversely, she was mortified when he nodded coolly, as though making love to her was something he could quite happily take or leave, and started the engine again.

'You don't mind?' she asked stiffly, her face burning.

'I'm devastated.' His voice was light, mocking, and the dark profile gave nothing away as she glanced at him. 'But I'll survive.'

The powerful and comfortable Range Rover made short work of the seventy or so miles to Fez, and, after stopping *en route* for an early lunch, they arrived at Morocco's most colourful ancient city in the early afternoon when the air was hot and languid.

They made their way to the older city, founded almost twelve hundred years ago and separated from the newer, modern European section by a muddy but life-giving river, and joined the throng streaming through the huge gates in the walls of the old city.

Marianne was enchanted by what she saw—robed Berbers and Arabs in turbans and burnouses, veiled women, hordes of bright-eyed children, flocks of sheep and goats, pack animals laden with bales of goods, and even an occasional water cart. It was like stepping back a thousand years in time, and she took photograph after photograph as more sights met her fascinated eyes.

'Keith would have loved this.' She meant nothing more by the remark than that Keith's artistic flair would have thoroughly appreciated and revelled in the wonderful pictures in front of them, but Hudson's face chilled at the mention of the other man's name.

'Then I'm heartbroken he's not here to see it,' he drawled with caustic sarcasm, his mouth hardening and his eyes cold.

'I only meant—' She stopped abruptly. She didn't have to explain herself to Hudson and she didn't intend to, she thought militantly. It was *he* who had manoeuvred *her* presence on this trip, without any consideration of what she wanted at all. She was blowed if she was going to start apologising for an innocent enough comment. 'Have you already reserved accommodation?' she asked tightly. 'It looks very busy.'

'Fez is a commercial centre as well as sometimes being referred to as the centre of Moroccan thinking,' Hudson said evenly, without replying to her question about accommodation. 'There are many schools here, as well as the Karouine University which is more than one thousand years old and famed throughout the Moslem world, so it's always a hive of activity with students and suchlike.'

'It's fascinating.' She eyed him determinedly. 'You've booked something in advance, then?' she pressed again.

'Yes, I've booked something in advance, Annie.'

He didn't elaborate, and some perverse little niggle compounded of pride and anger wouldn't let her enquire further. He had expected her to sleep with him—the seduction scene back in the Range Rover outside Tangier had proved that—but that was one thing she *wouldn't* be persuaded into. He'd already made it clear that in his reckoning she owed him for letting him down so badly, and this was obviously the time he intended to collect. Well—tough. She was here as his travelling companion, nothing more. He didn't love her, he didn't even seem to *like* her, and if he thought that she—

'You'll frighten the camels if you glare at them like that.'

'What?' She turned to glance his way as the deep, darkly amused voice spoke again. 'What did you say?'

'That frown is giving you a gargoyle fierceness that could well start a stampede,' he murmured imperturbably, indicating a group of tethered camels outside the car window. 'Have pity on them.'

'I was not frowning,' she protested quickly, ignoring his sceptical shake of the head and turning to stare at the vibrant scene outside the Range Rover. 'I was just looking, that's all.'

'That's your *normal* sightseeing face?' he asked in mock horror.

'And, even if I was, I don't intend to allow anyone to tell me not to,' Marianne stated firmly. 'My face is my own business.'

'Anyone' smiled lazily before drawing into a parking space and switching off the engine. 'A little walk will make you feel better,' Hudson said comfortingly, in the tone one used to deal with a tired and fractious child who was being deliberately difficult.

Marianne gritted her teeth. 'I'm fine, thank you, but a walk would be lovely.' She was quite pleased with the coolness of her voice.

'You look very beautiful in virginal white with your hair loose and your face freshly scrubbed; have I told you that?' he asked huskily, his voice dropping an octave or two and the warm, heady fragrance of him reaching out to entrap her as he leant across and touched the silken curls. 'Like a fallen angel.'

'A fallen angel? I hardly think so,' Marianne responded quickly.

'A green-eyed, rumpled, sexy angel,' he continued thickly, 'with the body of a goddess and a certain way of looking at a man that sets him on fire and makes him imagine—' He stopped abruptly.

'What?' she asked with breathless nervousness.

'How it would be.' His fingers entwined further into her hair, moving her head forward until her face was a breath away from his, her lips half-open and her heart thudding crazily. 'How it would be in my bed, the shower, the back of my car, a cornfield— Hell, you've no idea of the places I've imagined, Annie. I don't even know if some of them are physically possible but it'd be fun trying. Do fallen angels ever think like that?' he murmured softly.

'Hudson, you said you wouldn't do this. You said—'

'I want to eat you alive, Annie. Ravish you, taste you, turn day to night and night to day until you're so full of me you can't take any more. And then I want to do it all over again.'

She shut her eyes at the dark enchantment his words called forth, and when she opened them again, their green depths shimmering, it was to see he had moved back slightly to look down into her face. 'But first you take a step of faith, and you're not there yet, are you?' he said softly. 'You don't trust me; you're afraid for some reason. I can read it in those great eyes of yours.'

Afraid? Yes, she was afraid, but for him—not herself. And she trusted him—she would trust him with her life—but she couldn't very well say so. He was a man of integrity, honour, courage. And although she had killed his love for her she knew his physical desire for her body was still very real, but she wasn't strong enough to give herself to him for a brief interlude and then walk away.

But she would have to. Those very qualities that made him the man he was also made him a target for the men Michael had been mixed up with, men who hated and feared—with good cause—the name of Hudson de Sance. Men who weren't worthy to lick his boots.

'So I'll wait.' He moved back further, his hands falling away from her face, but although she was free she sat in exactly the same position, her mind spinning. 'Until the time is right for me to take you,' he said with incredible matter-of-factness.

'I don't want you to,' she whispered softly.

'There's...there's no point in you waiting for something that's not going to happen.'

'I don't agree.' He was quite still. 'And it *will* happen.'

'Hudson, we are nothing to each other now; you said so yourself—we aren't even friends. Why...why complicate things like this? I don't understand why you wanted me to come here with you. There must be hundreds of women who would be only too pleased to leap into your bed,' she finished miserably.

'Thousands,' he agreed laconically, his eyes tight on her face.

'Then why bother with someone who...who doesn't want to?'

'Call it a whim if you like,' he said evenly.

Marianne's stomach clenched and she lowered her gaze to her lap, her soft mouth unconsciously tightening. A whim? She had been reduced to a whim in his life? But then, whose fault was that?

'But for now we'll take a stroll around a souk, perhaps explore some of the narrow alleys that thread the medina and find a keepsake we might like to take home, yes?'

The last few words were like a punch in the chest as it hit her, with devastating painfulness, that if Michael had never come into her life the home Hudson had mentioned would have been their marital one. She would have been his wife. *His wife.*

'Fine.' Her nod and smile were brittle and she didn't say any more—her acting ability only went so far.

'And please try to relax a little,' he said coolly. 'This is supposed to be a holiday, after all; you've finished working now. You are allowed to enjoy yourself.' His eyes challenged her to take up the gauntlet but she ignored the dark gaze that held a wicked glitter in its depths.

'I am enjoying myself,' she answered brightly. 'Very much.'

'If this is you enjoying yourself very much, I'd hate

to see you when you're making an effort,' he drawled sardonically. 'But, no matter, you'll relax. I'll make you,' he added silkily.

She ignored that too.

CHAPTER SIX

THEIR hotel had formerly been a magnificent palace, built some two hundred years before by a Grand Vizier—a chief adviser to the sultan—and approached through a gate in the city wall. It was just after five when Marianne and Hudson walked across a hot and dusty courtyard, and, after going down several flights of shaded stone steps, emerged into a cool garden where banana trees, vibrant bougainvillea vines and a riot of other flowering tropical plants flourished amid the gentle murmur of several small stone fountains.

At the far end of the garden they passed through an imposing Moorish arch and into Reception, where a small and very charming Moroccan girl greeted them prettily, speaking quietly in perfect English with just the faintest trace of an accent.

Marianne had had all afternoon to think about her plan of action when the double room, or suite of rooms, was mentioned. She would be cool and firm, polite, but quite adamant when she made it clear she was insisting on her own quarters.

'Mr de Sance.' Hudson smiled at the receptionist, his handsome face portraying none of the agitation that was turning Marianne's stomach into a churning cauldron at the coming confrontation. 'I have made a reservation.'

She knew it. She had known it all along. One room.

'Ah, yes, Mr de Sance.' The girl smiled back, clearly thoroughly appreciating every inch of the lean, finely honed body in front of her. 'We have been expecting you both. A table for dinner has been reserved in your name and it is entirely up to you when you eat, but dinner is served from seven o'clock onwards...'

101

As the receptionist continued to give the practised speech, her voice soft and welcoming and the dark brown eyes flirtatious, Marianne nerved herself for the moment it would finish. How dared he, how *dared* he just assume she would fall into his hands like an overripe peach at the first opportunity? She hadn't seen him for two years, for goodness' sake. Did he really think she was that easy? Anyone would think they had just seen each other last week!

Two years—and whose fault is that? The inner voice spoke with devastating clarity and she felt a moment of searing guilt before she answered silently, Not mine, not really; it *isn't*.

But Hudson doesn't know that. Again it intruded when she least needed it, and now her reply was sharp and strong when she thought, Too late, it's done. And it's for the best—for him anyway.

'The bellboy will show you to your suites if you're ready?'

Marianne heard the last sentence through the turmoil in her mind, but indistinctly, like a faint drone. 'Did you say suites?' she asked carefully, vitally aware of Hudson at the side of her as she spoke directly to the girl, her voice quiet.

'Yes.' There was a moment's pause as the receptionist's dark eyes flickered towards Hudson. 'This is right, is it not? Two suites overlooking the city? This is what you required?'

'Perfect.' He turned to Marianne now, his eyes wicked as he added, 'Just perfect, wouldn't you say, Annie?'

'I... Yes—yes, of course—' She stopped the stammering abruptly. He had known exactly what she was thinking and he'd set her up for this embarrassing episode, she thought irritably. He was always one—no, ten, a hundred—steps in front of her, and there wasn't a darn thing she could do about it.

'Good.' All mockery had died from his eyes and his mouth was straight, almost grim, as he gave her one last

look before turning to where the bellboy was standing
waiting with their cases. Marianne didn't know what had
wiped the amusement from his countenance and at that
moment she found she didn't care; all her emotions were
taken up with the fact that Hudson hadn't intended to
share a room or a suite with her. It hurt. Ridiculously,
it hurt.

She knew it was unreasonable—if he had suggested
it she had been all ready to refuse—but the fact that he
hadn't wanted to had hit her hard. And she didn't like
that either.

The two suites were next to each other, and as the
bellboy opened the door leading to Marianne's lavishly
decorated rooms she couldn't stop her gasp of surprise.
The large sitting room was gloriously opulent, the walls
draped with rich swirls of dark green and turquoise silk
and the low cream divans scattered with piled cushions
of the same material. It had the appearance of a princely
desert tent, and the effect was continued through into the
beautiful bedroom, its sunken bed and exquisite furnish-
ings leaving her breathless. Arabian Nights in miniature.

What on earth did a suite like this cost a night? she
asked herself as she peered in at the sumptuous bathroom, which was all marble and mirrors. She couldn't
let Hudson pay, but she didn't know if she could afford
to pay either! She just hadn't expected anything like this.
She sat down rather suddenly on one of the divans as
the bellboy led Hudson to his own suite, and was still
sitting there in a daze some moments later when a knock
came at the door, and had to force herself to get up and
answer it.

'Dinner at eight?' Hudson was leaning against the
stone wall of the corridor when she opened the door, his
big, lean body indolent and relaxed and his eyes hooded
as he surveyed her on the threshold. 'That will give you
time to bathe and rest before we eat.'

'Hudson, how much is this hotel costing?' she asked
abruptly, her agitation doing away with any finesse.

'Why? Don't you like it?' His hands were thrust in his pockets, the material tight over his hips, and the very masculine posture did nothing for her composure or her pulse rate.

'I think it's gorgeous, but it must be very expensive,' she said a trifle breathlessly. 'You pay a fortune for this sort of ambience.'

'Do you?' he drawled easily. 'I wouldn't have said so.'

'Hudson, I want to know how much it is,' she insisted.

'Annie, why worry about the cost? I thought you realised all that was covered,' he said as he levered himself off the wall. 'We're on the road again tomorrow; it's just for one night.'

'You're not paying for me as well as yourself if that's what "covered" means,' she said firmly. 'I intended to do this trip, you know I did, and I'd put money aside for expenses and so on—'

'Which now won't be needed,' he cut in smoothly. 'End of story.'

'Hudson, there's no way I'd agree to you carrying all the expense; I never imagined you'd think I would. I think even a date should be fifty-fifty, let alone a trip like this.'

'Do you?' It was resigned and a trifle weary. 'I suppose I might have guessed, you being such a thoroughly modern woman, but we never got round to little things like that two years ago, did we? We were too occupied with other things.' A sardonic eyebrow quirked, but she was determined not to give in and stared back at him without smiling. 'Well, sorry to disappoint you but I'm old-fashioned enough to believe that certain things never change,' he continued easily, although she noticed a touch of steel in the cool voice now. 'And paying for the lady is one of them.'

'I'm not a lady—well, not in that sense,' she added quickly as the eyebrow rose higher. 'I'm a companion, the same as a man. Think of me like that if it makes it easier,' she said stoutly.

'Annie, sweetheart, whatever else, I could never think of you as a man,' he said with extreme dryness. 'And I am not prepared to argue with you on this. For once, *just once*,' he emphasised softly, 'don't fight me. Accept defeat gracefully...please?'

'I don't want to fight you—'

'Good, that's settled, then,' he cut in immediately.

'But I can't agree to this,' she continued irritably, ignoring the interruption as though he hadn't spoken. 'Surely you can see my point of view? It puts me under an...obligation. I don't like it.'

He looked at her for a long moment, his shirt open at the dark bronze of his neck and the lethal eyes narrowed on her troubled face, and the magnetism that was an essential part of his brooding attraction touched her senses, causing her to shiver deep inside.

'Annie, Annie...' He reached out and caught her wrist, drawing her towards him. 'There's not one other woman of my acquaintance who would really mean what you've just said. They might voice it for appearances' sake, the requisite social nicety, but they wouldn't object *too* hard,' he said with the touch of cynicism that was habitual with him, 'in case I took them at their word.'

'I mean it.' She wanted her voice to sound firm and controlled but it failed her miserably. 'I can assure you I mean it.'

'I know you do,' he said softly. 'And it's very nice of you.'

'So you agree?' she said quickly. 'I'll pay my half?'

'No.' He was suddenly very quiet, his face serious as he said, 'This is a brief sojourn out of real life—an illusion, a fantasy. Don't spoil it, Annie. Just...go with the flow.'

His lips covered hers as he pressed her back against the wall, his powerful body taut and hard as his hands moved over her softness and his mouth plundered hers.

The embrace was so unexpected, and so pleasurable, that she couldn't stop the gasping little whimper that escaped her throat, and as he heard the unmistakable sound of her desire he growled softly, the reverberation primitive and rough. The moment lengthened, stretching into pleasurable minutes.

His mouth searched hers intimately as his hands lowered to her hips, moving her against him in a way that fanned the flames of passion into a raging inferno for them both. 'Annie... What you do to me...' His voice was deep and husky, and she had no defence against it or the magic of his lovemaking. 'I only have to touch you and you turn to fire in my arms. How can you deny us both...?' he murmured softly. 'It's too cruel.'

'Hudson, stop...' Her voice was a shaken whisper as she twisted in his arms, and she could feel his heart pounding with the force of his desire when he kissed her again—deeply, intimately, until it was a kind of consummation in itself, the thrust of his tongue erotic and savage until she pushed frantically against him.

This time he stopped—his mouth tearing away from hers with a groan that was echoed in the heart of her. He was breathing hard, his massive chest rising and falling for long moments under the thin material of his shirt as he fought for control. He let her go slowly, placing his hands on the wall, his arms outstretched and his head hanging down as she backed away from him into her room and shut the door with hands that trembled.

Dinner was a painful affair for Marianne—at least at first. Hudson had dressed up as befitted the superior restaurant—resplendent in black dinner jacket and tie—and when she opened her door to his knock at five minutes to eight she went weak at the knees at the sight of him.

'You look very lovely,' he said softly, taking her arm in a manner so relaxed and natural that if she hadn't known the heated episode of a couple of hours ago had definitely taken place she would have thought she'd imagined it. 'Very lovely indeed.'

'Thank you.' Her voice was shaking but for the life of her she couldn't match his cool control. She had dressed carefully for the evening ahead, knowing she needed every little bit of help she could get to appear composed and unruffled. Her above-the-knee, long-sleeved, high-necked cocktail dress in a pale shade of green was made of a silky-soft material that clung in all the right places, but at the same time kept everything covered. She really couldn't have faced having an inch of skin exposed to Hudson's dark gaze that night, although she knew it was foolish of her.

However, Marianne was completely unaware of the provocativeness of the demure style when linked with the soft, clinging silk, and the fact that it was far more sexy to the discerning male than any blatant show of flesh. And Hudson was a discerning male...

She was overwhelmingly thankful for the two cocktails they enjoyed in the little bar off Reception. The pale amber liquid looked innocuous enough but had the kick of a mule, and enabled her to respond to Hudson's conversation more or less coherently, in spite of the whirling agitation and panic that the big, dark body induced without any effort at all.

By the time they walked through to the restaurant she had begun to relax, and as Hudson chatted over their first course, his conversation easy and inconsequential, she relaxed still more. By the time dessert was served Marianne had realised she was actually enjoying herself, and it was all due to Hudson. He had set himself out to be amusing and non-threatening, teasing her, making her laugh, his air one of lazy comfortableness.

'Oh, I love all the pastries they do out here,' Marianne said happily, digging her spoon into the layers of thin, flaky crust held together with cream, fruit and thick syrup with childish satisfaction, and closing her eyes for a moment at the first taste. 'They're gorgeous, just gorgeous.'

Damn it, how he wanted her... Hudson's loins tightened as he watched her small pink tongue lick a morsel of pastry from the corner of her mouth, the action sensuous and cat-like. She was relaxed now—she had been like a cat on a hot tin roof when she'd first opened the door—but one wrong move from him and that formidable drawbridge would be hoisted into place. He wanted her, he intended to have her, but only when the time was right. He'd waited two years to possess her; he could wait a while longer—in spite of the battering his ego took every time they connected.

What was it about him that she found so hard to take anyway? he felt the familiar rage and bitterness begin to flavour the moment and forced them back into the dark recesses of his mind. No matter. He was trained in breaking down defences and getting what he wanted, and time and circumstances were on his side. He only had to be patient. The word mocked him.

'You'll get fat.' His smile was amiable and soothing, his eyes hooded as he watched her finish the dessert, and again, as she licked the spoon clean, he felt his loins stir.

'I know.' She smiled back, the cocktails and two glasses of wine she had consumed with the meal mellowing her voice. 'I don't care. I'm one of those people who live to eat, not eat to live.'

'Dangerous talk.' He leant forward, tilting her small chin with his large hand as he said, 'No signs of a double chin yet, but beware the demon pastries.' His fingers lingered on the velvety-soft skin for a second longer than was necessary, before they moved caressingly across her throat and brushed the pale green silk as they reluctantly left, but when her startled green eyes met his, his expression was mild and benign, even tranquil.

She smiled again, but nervously this time, her confusion evident in the slight flush in her cheeks and rapid pulse in the silky skin he had just touched. 'You...you don't like plump women, then?' she asked with forced lightness.

'I didn't say that.' His eyes were smoky and as dark as charcoal. 'I have no particular leaning one way or the other beyond that they are blonde—a pale, golden sort of blonde—with emerald-green eyes that hold flecks of sunlight in the depths of them, and a mouth…a mouth that begs to be kissed,' he finished huskily, his gaze moving to her lips where it caressed her skin lingeringly.

She stared at him, utterly unable to reply.

He held her gaze, his eyes moving to capture hers and his face still and quiet, his body tense for one long moment before he shrugged coolly, breaking the spell. 'Other than that I'm not fussy,' he said mockingly.

Marianne lingered over coffee, less because of her appreciation of the aromatic brew than because of the fact that in a few minutes she was going to have to let Hudson see her to her suite, and then… What? she asked herself despairingly. That had been a seduction speech if ever she'd heard one, and the trouble was he was so good at it. She should never have had those cocktails and glasses of wine—she needed every bit of thinking power when she was in his company.

'There's no more in the pot.' As her hand reached for the coffee pot to pour another—her fourth—cup, Hudson's voice was dark and soft. 'Would you like me to call the waiter for a refill? Although all that caffeine will make it hard to sleep.'

'Oh, no, no, I've…I've had enough.' She had, more than enough—in fact the last cup had had to be forced down in tiny gulps—but the coffee was all she had as a delaying tactic.

'You really do like the Moroccan coffee, don't you?' Hudson said with innocent observation. 'It's no trouble to get more—'

'No really.' The four cups of the rich, thick infusion were already beginning to swish about in her over-full stomach with more gusto than she would have liked, and

she had a nasty feeling that Hudson had seen her pro-
crastination for what it was. 'I've had enough.'

He put his arm round her waist as they left the table—his fingers splaying on the soft swell of her stomach with burning heat—and she couldn't believe what
the feel of the masculine body did to hers. She shivered,
and then took an iron grip on herself to prevent another
such occurrence. What was the matter with her, for
goodness' sake? she asked herself crossly. Anyone
would think she was a nervous teenager on her first date,
although arguably most of the teenagers she met these
days probably knew far more about a man's body than
she did.

She stumbled slightly as they walked down the marble
steps leading from the restaurant, and immediately his
arm tightened before drawing her into the protection of
his hard frame and he said, 'Careful, sweetheart,' his
voice deep and soft.

She wished he wouldn't call her that. No doubt it was
his stock address to all the women he took into his bed—
part of the overall seduction technique—and as such it
rankled, fiercely.

'I'm fine, thank you.' Her voice was prim as she carefully moved herself out of his hold, but the hectic flush
in her cheeks and over-bright eyes told their own story.
'You don't need to—'

'What's wrong with my putting my arm round you?'
he asked easily as he pulled her close again. 'And who
said anything about need? Perhaps I *like* to hold you.
What's wrong with that?'

'There's nothing wrong with it, but I don't think—'

'Perhaps you like me to hold you,' he added softly.
'Do you, Annie? Do you like to feel the warmth of my
skin against yours? To feel the way you fit into my side
like you were made to be there? A delicious, living jig-
saw...'

'This is a silly conversation.' There was a riot in her
stomach now that had nothing to do with the coffee.

'Why? Because we're talking about sex?' He said the word as though it were nothing at all, and Marianne almost missed her step again. 'Why are you afraid of me, Annie? Is it me or all men? What's happened to make you so scared? Is it the emotional commitment or the act itself? Are you afraid I'd be too rough, too big, that I'd hurt you—?'

'*Hudson!*'

She jerked away, glancing round hastily to see if any-one could have overheard them, her cheeks scarlet with embarrassment.

'You haven't answered my question,' he persisted re-lentlessly.

'Nor am I going to,' she said stiffly, although tucked into his side as she was her voice carried less censure than she would have liked. 'To answer it would give credence to the idea that I'm frightened of you, which is too ridiculous for words. Just because I don't...I don't offer myself to everyone,' she continued feverishly, 'doesn't mean I'm scared of men. I have principles—'

'So do I,' he said seriously, glancing down at her briefly.

'There you are, then. You can understand what I mean.'

'But there is an enormous difference between having principles and living the life of a nun, Annie. Five and five doesn't add up to ten with you, and that...irritates me.' He turned her round, bringing her into the circle of his arms as they reached her suite, and then backing her against the wall as he looked down at her with dark, narrowed eyes. 'And puzzles me too,' he admitted thoughtfully. 'And it's a failing of mine that I always have to solve puzzles.'

'I do apologise for disturbing that illustrious brain.' The sarcasm didn't quite come off, trapped as she was by his big male body, and enveloped by the warmth and smell of him. 'If I irritate you so much—' the word had

rankled '—why did you insist that we travel together?'
she asked tightly.

'Damned if I know.' His eyes narrowed further. 'Perhaps I'm a glutton for punishment? It could be that; I
was always stubborn and awkward even as a child. Or
maybe it's a matter of unfinished business. That's another thing that has always had the power to get to me.
Or it could even be that any company is better than no
company at all.' He smiled mockingly.

'Charming.' She tried to glare at him but the anger
his words had induced was watered down by the potent
magnetism of his nearness, and the word sounded humiliatingly breathless.

'You did ask.' He stared down into her face for one
more moment, his eyes moving over her hair, her eyes,
the silky-smooth skin with its delicate blush of pink, and
then he reached out and touched her mouth with his
finger, tracing the outline of her lips with a sensual caress. 'Goodnight, Annie.' And then he straightened up
with an abruptness that left her stunned as he turned and
walked away.

The cool control Hudson displayed that evening characterised his dealings with Marianne over the next few
days. They left Fez early the next morning when it was
still relatively cool, arriving in modern Rabat's broad,
flower-lined streets later that day, and exploring its ancient medina the next morning before it got too hot.

Hudson was charming but faintly remote, teasing her
a little—as a niece could expect from a favourite uncle—but maintaining a detachment that made Marianne
feel quite isolated at times. And so it continued, even
when, on the third night of the trip, Hudson escorted her
to a wildly exotic nightclub in Casablanca and Marianne
found herself trying to provoke something more. The
very moment she realised what she was doing she
stopped, but it hadn't made any difference anyway—he
was still the benevolent uncle figure, and it was driving

her mad. She told herself she was being inconsistent, selfish, unreasonable—that it was far better he viewed her platonically; it was what she had demanded after all. But in spite of her acknowledgement of her fallaciousness it still hurt.

They arrived in Marrakesh late in the afternoon of the fifth day, and by then Marianne was convinced that any attraction Hudson might still have harboured towards her had been well and truly dealt with by that formidable mind.

The city had a special charm of its own that was undeniably romantic, many of its streets being lined with orange trees and gardens filled with bougainvillea and flowering jasmine that perfumed the air with a sweet odour, and Marrakesh itself being surrounded by orchards of olive trees and date palms bearing heavy bunches of fruit high in the air.

Marianne found its location—lying in the foothills of the High Atlas Mountains due south of Casablanca—fascinatingly picturesque, the reservoirs made by damming streams in the mountains nearby providing a lushness to the city that had been missing elsewhere. But Hudson seemed quite unmoved by the romance in the air.

It would be a wonderful place for a honeymoon... The thought shocked her and she glanced quickly at Hudson, big and dark beside her, as they drove past medieval palaces and other ancient and beautiful buildings towards the large square called Djemaa-el-Fna, deep inside the medina, where there was a fair beginning at about four every afternoon.

'Idris made me promise to pay a visit,' Hudson had said earlier with a wry smile as they'd been approaching the city, and he had told Marianne about the famous fair. 'He was horrified we might just come to Marrakesh without visiting Djemaa-el-Fna.' And so, on their arrival at 'the gateway to the south', they had parked the Range Rover outside the rosy pink medina wall, whereupon they had hired one of the hundreds of horse-drawn gigs lined along its length, and were now being driven in style to the great square.

It was alive with what seemed to Marianne's fascinated eyes thousands of people waiting to be entertained when they arrived just before four, and, after Hudson had paid the Arab who had driven them his required fee, he took her small hand in his.

'I wanted to show you the real Morocco when you came on this trip,' he said softly, his eyes warmer than they had been in days. 'And this is part of it. Let's just enjoy it together.'

'But the hotel? They won't let our rooms go?' Marianne asked anxiously. 'It might be late when we leave.'

'It's okay.' He smiled, drawing her close and kissing the tip of her nose in a light caress before adding, 'I know the owner.'

She couldn't argue any more; her heart was singing suddenly at the look in his eyes after the days of coolness, even as she berated herself for her stupidity. She had to be careful—doubly careful—when he was like this. She couldn't afford to let her guard down for a moment. She loved him too much to get careless.

Marianne knew, as the afternoon stretched into evening, that she was going to remember the bitter-sweet enchantment of the hours spent with Hudson for the rest of her life. They listened to story-tellers, watched snake-charmers, magicians, jugglers and agile acrobats parade their skills, and the inevitable medicine men demonstrate the miraculous cures in their brightly coloured bottles.

There were many cooks tending their braziers while they grilled succulent pieces of fish or chunks of meat, and as the light began to fade into an aromatic dusk Hudson and Marianne ate charcoaled fish and sweet Moroccan bread washed down with bottled water, followed by handfuls of dried figs and dates.

It was a step outside real life—a dream, a taste of

what might have been—and all the more poignant because of it.

'Worth coming?' Hudson's voice was soft as they stood finishing the last of the dates and watching the vendors beginning to pack up their wares as the dark shadows of night encroached on the colourful scene, blanketing it in a velvety dusk.

'Definitely.' And it had been—if only because of the magical bubble that had enclosed them as they had wandered hand in hand about the square like any other couple on holiday.

'Come on; we'll find a taxi to take us back to the Range Rover,' Hudson said quietly, and he slipped an arm about her waist, pulling her into the side of him as they turned to retrace their footsteps.

He kept his arm round her during the drive back, but although there were times—many times—when Marianne thought he was going to kiss her he didn't, much to her increasing chagrin.

The Range Rover was where they had left it, and once inside Hudson started the engine without attempting to touch her, his face cool and expressionless and his hands steady. They drove to the modern part of the city, built about one and a half miles from the old medina, and into a wide, tree-lined street where large houses reposed in regal splendour, surrounded by their own grounds and flower-filled gardens. It was the haunt of the wealthy.

'Oh.' Marianne glanced about her as Hudson cut the engine after drawing into one of the drives and stopping in front of a long, low, sprawling residence of some distinction. 'Have…have you a call to make or something?'

'Something, actually.' His face was still cool as he turned to face her and she knew instantly she wasn't going to like what he was going to say, and steeled herself for what was to come.

'This is the part of Marrakesh where Hassan, Idris's

brother, lives,' Hudson said quietly. 'They're expecting us.'

'Who's expecting us?' Marianne asked suspiciously.

'Hassan and his wife.' It was said with studied patience.

'You didn't tell me Idris's brother lived in Marrakesh.' Marianne slanted her eyes at him in the shadowed drive but could read nothing from the poker-face in front of her. 'They're expecting us for a meal, is that it? But won't they have assumed we'd go to our hotel and change first? And I couldn't eat anything, not after all that food at the fair,' she added quickly.

'You won't have to eat anything.' Hudson eyed her steadily.

She didn't trust him when he was quiet and patient—like now. 'What does that mean?' she asked doubtfully.

'They've offered to put us up for the night, that's all,' Hudson drawled easily. 'Idris happened to mention to Hassan we were coming this way, and Hassan would have considered it the gravest insult if we had gone to a hotel. Moroccans are tremendously hospitable,' he added—so innocently that Marianne's qualms intensified. 'They take such things very seriously.'

She stared at him for a long moment before saying flatly, 'Why didn't you tell me we weren't staying at a hotel?'

'Is it important?' he countered evenly. 'It's just for a night.'

'I think so.' She drew back slightly in her seat to survey him better. 'It makes me wonder what else you haven't told me.'

'Don't make this into a drama, Annie,' he said coolly, immediately making her feel ridiculous for having objected. 'And, if we're talking about who hasn't told who what, I hardly think you're in a position to object to anything I might have done, do you?' He looked at her sardonically, his gaze cold.

'That's not fair.' She knew she was blushing and it made her voice sharp.

'On the contrary,' he said tightly, a touch of ice chilling the deep tones. 'It's damn fair. Now, it's late and Hassan is expecting us, so if you're ready...?'

He left the vehicle before she could reply, walking round the bonnet and opening her door as she sat quietly seething at his high-handedness. She glanced at his outstretched hand without moving, and then raised her gaze slowly to his where their eyes met and held for a full thirty seconds.

Fait accompli, she told herself irritably as she registered iron in the inflexibility of the grey gaze. It was too late to change things now, and there was no valid reason to do so anyway besides a gut feeling she couldn't explain. But this was all too... She balked at the word 'intimate' and substituted 'cosy' instead. A hotel was neutral somehow; she still had control over things in that environment. But as Idris's brother's guest...

She climbed out of the Range Rover without availing herself of Hudson's help—earning an exasperated frown in the process—and kept her head high and her back straight as Hudson pulled their cases out before walking across the pebbled drive to the ornate front door.

He didn't look to see if she was behind him, although her feet on the scrunchy stones probably told him she was, and again his male arrogance rankled, as did his next words... 'I trust you don't intend to make a scene in front of Hassan and his wife?' he asked as he turned to face her at last.

'Of course I don't.' She glared at him, her eyes fiery. 'It's very kind of them to offer us beds for the night; I just hope it hasn't put them out too much.'

'Receiving guests runs in the blood of most Moroccans,' Hudson said coolly. 'They are a very gracious people.' There was an inflexion in the deep voice, just the merest something, that insinuated he did not consider that attribute to be one of her virtues, but as he swung round and rang the bell in that instant the chance to challenge him on it was lost. Which was probably just as well.

The door was opened almost immediately—with a swiftness that suggested the occupants were already aware of their arrival—and the man standing there was so like Idris it could only be Hassan, his brother. They were more like twins than mere brothers.

'Hudson, my friend.' Hassan's smile was wide and gold-toothed. 'Welcome, welcome. And this must be your Annie, yes? She is even more beautiful than Idris led me to believe. Come in, come in. Kalia is waiting to meet you both.'

'Your Annie'? There wasn't time to dwell on Hassan's words, but the portent in them was at the back of Marianne's mind during all the introductions to Hassan and his delightful family, and the hour following when they sat talking and drinking cups of the very sweet green tea flavoured with mint that the Moroccans favoured.

Hassan and Kalia were treating her as Hudson's girlfriend—it became more and more apparent as the hour progressed—but, other than cutting into the conversation and making a definite statement to the contrary, Marianne really didn't know how to dissuade them of the notion. She tried a couple of tactful hints, the implication of which seemed to pass unnoticed, but as Hudson himself was giving credence to their supposition—more by what was unsaid than said—she finally admitted defeat and decided to let them think what they liked.

They were Hudson's friends, after all—she would probably never see them again in her life—and if he wanted Hassan and Kalia to think they were a couple she really didn't see the harm in it. Until they were shown to their sleeping quarters, that was.

'I hope you will find your rooms comfortable.' Hassan smiled and nodded as the little maid who had served them all tea gestured for them to follow her. 'Please tell

Sorai if there is anything you need. It is our desire that your stay be comfortable.'

Rooms. Marianne expelled a silent sigh of relief as she and Hudson followed the slim girl who, unlike her employers, wore traditional Moroccan dress. As the minutes had lengthened she had begun to have the suspicion—unworthy now, she recognised with a little stab of guilt—that Hudson had his own, distinctly carnal reasons for allowing Hassan and Kalia to assume they were a couple. That would teach her to keep her imagination under control.

'What's this?'

The maid had opened the door to a suite of rooms—in which Marianne had assumed there would be two bedrooms—and left, after showing them the bell-cord in case they required anything.

'A bedroom?' Hudson suggested lazily, glancing round the sumptuous room appreciatively. 'Rather a nice one too, I might add.'

But...' Marianne stared aghast at the most enormous bed she had ever seen in her life. 'Where's the other bedroom?

'You don't think there's room there for two?' Hudson asked with mock incredulity, although if she had been looking his way—rather than staring transfixed at the huge bed—she would have seen his eyes had narrowed intently on her shocked face. 'This suite already has a bathroom that would hold a baseball team, plus a sitting room; what else do you expect?'

'My own bed.' Her eyes turned to his. 'I'm not sleeping in that with you,' she stated with bald directness, her fiery face belying the flatness of her tone. 'I'll ring for Sorai.'

As she turned to step back into the small sitting room the maid had first shown them into Hudson caught her wrist, swinging her back to face him. 'The hell you are.' It was a soft growl, but Marianne was too angry to be intimidated. 'You can't embarrass Hassan by insulting him like that.'

'What about the insult to me, then?' Marianne shot back furiously. 'You led them both to believe I was your…your—'

'What?' he asked coldly. 'Spit it out.'

'Mistress!' She glared at him.

'Of course I didn't; don't be so ridiculous,' he said frostily.

'Then how do you explain that?' She gestured wildly towards the gargantuan bed, complete with silk covers, scattered pillows, cushions and the sort of appeal that shouted 'love-nest'.

'Marianne, I had no idea Hassan would assume we were sleeping together,' Hudson said icily, his use of her full name an indication that the outward calm was merely a façade to mask the anger within. 'But even though he has it is hardly an insult. He knows we were together once and has naturally assumed we're more than friends.'

'Oh, and every woman you're "together" with, you sleep with, is that it?' she snapped back angrily. 'How many other girls have you brought here—?'

'That's enough.' His voice and his face were icy now.

She was too enraged to heed the warning. 'I can see it all now,' she spat hotly. 'I thought it was all too pat, too convenient. What went wrong? Did she back out at the last minute? But of course, she must have done. What was it, work commitments? Or did you have a row? And you had the cheek to assume I'd fall in with your plans!'

'I don't have the faintest idea what you are talking about,' Hudson said with a softness that should have told her something.

'That woman, the redhead,' she spat furiously. 'The one who was all over you at the hotel.' She remembered her name perfectly well, but she was blowed if she was going to give him further satisfaction by revealing that—she'd said too much already.

It appeared Hudson agreed with her.

'My relationship with Jasmine is nothing to do with you.' It was deadly—the same sort of cold, analytical frostiness he used with such effect in his work when he wanted to devastate and destroy. 'But before you cast aspersions on her character I'd mention that to my knowledge she has never set someone up for a fall, unlike some.'

'Meaning?' His championship of the other woman cut her to the quick. 'Don't stop there—say exactly what you mean.'

'You really want me to spell it out?' he said grimly.

'I hate you.' And she did, right at that moment.

'Possibly.' He considered her burning face with stony grey eyes. 'But believe me, Annie, you can't feel anything for me I haven't felt ten-fold for you. There was a time, when you first left and I imagined you with him, that I wanted to kill you.' As her eyes widened he nodded slowly. 'Oh, yes, it's true,' he affirmed with silky savagery. 'You get to hear a lot of things in my work, meet a lot of people that aren't nice to know, and for a time I really thought about it. If I could have found you both then...'

She shivered as he paused, surveying him with eyes that fear had turned jade-green, her face chalk-white.

'But you had covered your tracks too well,' he continued softly, 'and so I waited, biding my time, knowing that one day our paths would cross again.' He nodded slowly. 'And they did.'

'How did you know?' she whispered, trembling. 'That we'd meet?'

'Because I never give up,' he said with chilling matter-of-factness. 'It's not in my nature to accept defeat.'

'What...what are you going to do?' She had never felt so paralysingly scared in her life. She had heard of women who had said—after having been attacked or threatened—that they had been too frightened to move, but she had always dismissed such statements as exaggeration. But she was experiencing it now, her limbs rigid with fright and her brain numb. She was frozen before him.

'Do?' A strange expression flicked over his face for a second as he saw her fear. 'I'm going to do nothing, Annie,' he said quietly, his body as tense as hers. 'I could never hurt you, I knew that all along, but it didn't help in the initial pain and humiliation to acknowledge it. The guy might have been a different matter...' He nodded slowly. '*Would* have been,' he affirmed softly.

She continued to stare at him, her composure fragile.

'But that's all dead and gone now,' he said grimly as she still remained frozen in front of him, like a tiny rabbit in the headlights of a car. 'We've moved on, both of us. You have your exciting life, your career... Is it enough, Annie? In the chill of the night, when you can't sleep and there's no one there to stroke away the fears, the nightmares? And don't tell me you don't have them,' he added, 'because everyone does, even the toughest of us.' The silky voice was ruthless.

'I...I'm doing all right,' she stammered weakly.

'But I don't think you're tough, Annie.' He continued as though he hadn't heard her trembling whisper. 'I don't think you're tough at all. Don't ask me how I know, I just know, and I'd bet my life on it. Strange, really...' He paused again, but she could read nothing from the veiled eyes beyond a kind of thoughtful pensiveness. 'I feel so sure about that aspect, and yet everything you've done points to my being wrong. Am I wrong?' he asked suddenly, his voice and manner changing and shocking her out of the false security his words had lulled her into.

Oh, he was good, he was very, very good, Marianne thought desperately, recognising too late he had been using the same sort of tactics he applied with such brilliance in the courtroom.

She didn't reply immediately, forcing herself to take a few deep, calming breaths to steady her pounding heart and racing pulse, before she said, 'We...we weren't discussing me. I was objecting to you bringing me here and setting this up—'

'Objection noted.' His eyes narrowed, and he actually had the gall to smile as he added, 'You'd be a worthy adversary in court, Miss McBride-Harding. You don't get intimidated easily.'

'The name is Harding, and this isn't a game,' she bit back quickly, bitterly hurt that he could dismiss the crucifying pain he had brought to the surface so casually.

'I know that.' His voice was a whiplash. 'And just be glad you've got off so lightly. It's more than you deserve.'

'Lightly? When you're suggesting—?'

'I have no intention of leaping on you when you're asleep and ravaging your body,' he said coolly, and with such disgust that every bit of self-confidence she had shrivelled up and died. 'Believe it or not, I do actually know women who find my attentions welcome.' The bolt of jealousy she felt was so savage, it killed any retort. 'I have never taken anything that wasn't freely given.'

She didn't doubt that for a minute. There was probably one such woman kicking herself at this moment because she had been prevented from making the trip with him. A woman with red hair and the sort of come-hither smile that would never turn him away, a woman who was free to love him, with no skeletons in the cupboard and messy family traumas. Someone vibrant, uninhibited...

'Now, the bed is seven feet across if it's an inch,' Hudson continued evenly. 'I hardly think we're going to bump into each other by accident. However, if it makes you feel safer—' the sarcasm was caustic '—we can make it into two separate halves with some of those pillows.'

'I can sleep on the sofa in there.' She pointed through

the doorway to the neat sitting room where a brocade sofa reposed, along with matching easy chairs and a small television set.

'I don't think so.' He eyed her darkly. 'And there is no way I'm doing the gentlemanly thing and having a night of misery out there either. No, reconcile yourself to the bed,' he said with dry mockery. 'It'll only be for a few hours, after all.'

'I really don't think that's a good idea, and it's not because—'

'Just do it, Annie.' It was the voice of a man who had come to the end of his tether, and she recognised it as such.

'All right.' She felt raw and vulnerable and exposed, and his earlier words—about the other women, and Jasmine in particular—were eating away at her brain. It was one thing to make the supreme sacrifice and walk away when she knew she wasn't going to see him again, quite another to have him in the flesh in front of her and have all the nightmares and daytime images of Hudson with other women confirmed to her. *Quite another.*

From the second she had seen him again her love had grown stronger and stronger—its intensity heightened by the years of separation—and now the pain of it was fast becoming unbearable.

She should never have agreed to come on this trip—it had been madness, emotional suicide—and she knew, with dreadful and frightening clarity, that she was going to have to pay the price for her weakness. For wanting to be with him.

She loved him, she would die loving him, and the way she felt at this moment she wouldn't care if it was soon. But she could never let him know. And right at this minute she felt like the most pathetic creature in the world.

CHAPTER SEVEN

MARIANNE hid in the flamboyant bathroom as long as she dared after her shower, taking an age to dry her hair and then restraining the riotous tumble of silky gold curls in two tight plaits at either side of her head. Hudson had always liked her hair loose—finding it sexy—and the plaits served a dual purpose of hiding as much of the profusion of curls as possible and giving—she hoped—an impression of demure restraint. She stared in the mirror anxiously.

Her face was squeaky clean, and in spite of the sticky, warm night she had pulled her ankle-length towelling robe over her nightie, the only visible areas of skin her hands and feet. She pulled the belt even tighter before she opened the door, hoping Hudson would think the colour in her cheeks was due to the hot water rather than the embarrassing shyness that had made her as jumpy as a cricket.

'Finished?' He was sitting on the magnificent bed reading an official-looking document as she entered the bedroom, and she saw he had already set the barrier of heaped pillows into place. 'Just catching up on some background to a proposed change in the law,' he said idly as he flung the papers aside.

'Don't you ever stop working?'

'Oh, yes, Annie, when there's something more pleasant to do,' he murmured softly, straight-faced but wickedly amused at her confusion. 'There's nothing I like better than a spot of relaxing.'

She went hot inside, catching one bare foot in a luxuriant Moroccan rug as she padded across to the dressing table and nearly landing at Hudson's feet before she managed to save herself.

'The…the bathroom's free,' she said hastily.

'Thank you.' Again she heard the dark amusement he was trying to hide, and kept her eyes resolutely to the front as she sank down on the little upholstered stool in front of the dressing table and opened her pot of hand cream, her face flaming with embarrassment.

She was aware of the movement of his body as he stood up, and also that he had paused just behind her as he walked across the room, but when one caressing finger ran softly across the nape of her neck she nearly jumped out of her skin and she shot around.

'Steady, girl, steady,' he soothed irritatingly. 'I don't bite— Well, not often anyway,' he added with an exaggerated leer.

'Hudson—'

'Yes, Annie?' he interjected with suspicious meekness.

'Just get ready for bed.' It was the wrong thing to say, and immediately the words had left her lips she knew it—but he so *muddled* her, she thought helplessly, her senses screaming.

'Certainly,' he said politely. 'I thought you'd never ask.'

'And stop being…' There wasn't a word for the magnetic pull of that flagrant masculinity, and she stared up at him helplessly for a moment, her gaze faltering before the dark, glittering eyes.

'Yes?' he enquired helpfully. 'Stop being…?'

'Oh, nothing.' She tried to glare at him but it didn't come off.

He smiled, gently, and then continued towards the door, pausing for a moment as he turned to look at her again. 'It was a nice try but it didn't work,' he said softly.

'What?' She stared at him bewilderedly, her colour still high.

'The hair.' His gaze wandered over the plaits from which several little curls had escaped, the look in his eyes bringing a heat to her stomach that was a painful, pleasurable ache.

She shut her eyes for a moment before forcing steel into her gaze and glaring at him without saying a word.

'I'm going, I'm going...' He disappeared into the bathroom.

She had only brought a couple of whisper-thin nighties with her, knowing the nights would be warm, and although the one she was wearing was the more circumspect of the two its gossamer delicacy left nothing to the imagination, Marianne reflected uneasily.

Could she sleep in her robe? The sultriness of the night mocked the idea, but she could at least keep it on until she was under the covers. She'd have to, she decided desperately, and then sort of wriggle out of it and let it slide onto the floor. She'd do that once the light was out—the covers themselves were as fine as a spider's web.

She climbed into bed, wrapped the folds of the robe about her legs and pulled the covers around her waist, thereby dislodging the army of pillows which fell in all directions. By the time they were back in place and she was installed with a book in her side of the bed, Marianne had heard Hudson leave the bathroom.

She gazed feverishly at the book in her hands, the lines of black print dancing madly in front of her eyes, and tried to pretend she always lay in bed on a baking-hot night with enough nightwear on for the Antarctic. It appeared Hudson had no such scruples.

'That feels better,' he said contentedly.

She raised her eyes from the book to see him strolling round the end of the bed, dressed in nothing but a small—alarmingly small—towel wrapped snugly round his lean hips. And once Marianne looked she kept on looking—she couldn't help it.

His broad, muscled shoulders and wide, powerful

chest were gleaming in the muted light from the bedside lamps, and his chest was hairy—very hairy, Marianne thought as a trickle of something hot shivered down her spine. His legs and arms were hairy too, and on his chest the tight black curls suggested his head hair would be curly as well if he let it grow beyond its severely cropped style—perhaps that was why he didn't, she reflected shakily.

His thighs looked strong and hard, and he was very tanned, his skin dark against the snowy whiteness of the towel. Altogether it was a male body—overwhelmingly, menacingly male—that looked as finely honed as any athlete's, and it made Marianne feel even more jittery than she had been feeling.

Hudson glanced at her as he reached his side of the bed and she dropped her gaze quickly, mortifyingly aware that she had been ogling him, and that he knew. She could tell from the gleam of satisfaction in the slumberous, darkly sensual eyes.

'Cold?'

It was a lazy drawl and meant to provoke, but even with her eyes on the book all Marianne could see was a lithe, tanned, muscled body that would make any woman weak at the knees, and her voice reflected her own weakness as she said shakily, 'Not particularly.'

'Oh.' He continued to watch her without moving.

One little word, but it carried a wealth of meaning, and this time the adrenalin provided a welcome boost that made her voice sharp as she retorted, 'I'll take my robe off when I'm good and ready, thank you,' as she raised her head to glare at him.

'I told you, Annie, you've nothing to fear from me,' Hudson said gently. 'And I meant it.'

The ridiculousness of the statement hit her between the eyes as she found herself staring at him again, and she was conscious of the fact that she was desperately trying to keep her gaze fixed on his face and ignore the acres of bare flesh beneath. 'I didn't think I had,' she replied stiffly. And it genuinely wasn't Hudson's control she was worried about so much as her own. How was she going to manage to get through the night and keep her hands off him?

'Good.' He smiled, and she could have hit him. 'You'll have to excuse the towel,' he continued contentedly, 'but I don't possess a pair of pyjamas.'

'Oh.' Her colour increased and with it her agitation.

'And by some oversight I left my robe in Tangier.' He shrugged easily, the movement flexing powerful muscles and making her hot. 'No doubt they'll send it on.'

'No doubt.' *He was going to sleep naked?* He couldn't, could he?

'Good book?' He gestured innocently towards the novel in her hands, and she reflected that the towel looked frighteningly slack.

'What? Oh, yes, yes it is,' she agreed quickly.

'Perhaps it'd help if you...' He made a turning movement with his hands, his voice magnificently expressionless.

She hadn't! She hadn't been holding the thing upside down? She had. She prayed the bed would open and swallow her.

'Oh. I'd just dropped it. When you came in, I'd just dropped it and I must have...' Her voice trailed away as she realised she was babbling, and she forced herself to take a long, deep breath before she said, 'I'm ready for sleep now, anyway.'

'Me too.'

He dropped the towel with magnificent unconcern, and although Marianne kept her eyes glued frantically on his face she was agonisingly aware of the hair on his chest narrowing to a thin line before it flared out again between his thighs.

'Goodnight, then.' She shot round in the bed and slid down under the covers with her face flaming. He had been aroused. For all his easy talk and coolness, he had been aroused...

'Sweet dreams, Annie,' Hudson murmured huskily.

She smelt the clean, sharp tang of his aftershave as he slid into bed, and then heard him swear softly as the pillows tumbled with his entry under the sheets, but she didn't move to help him put them back into place, merely stretching out a careful hand and clicking off her bedside lamp. She heard him do the same, and then, as the room was plunged into darkness, lay stiff and rigid under the sheets as her blood surged through her veins and her senses screamed.

How in the world had she got herself into this impossible situation anyway? She wanted to cry and shout and scream, to bellow out her frustration and pain and the sheer hopelessness of it all, but she didn't. She lay quietly, each breath an effort of self-control, and stared into the blackness as she forced her pulse to slow. The air pressed down on her, sultry and sticky and thick.

After a few minutes she knew she would melt with the heat if she didn't slip the thick towelling robe off, so she carefully twisted in the bed, hoping Hudson wouldn't realise what she was doing, and pulled the heavy folds away from her body, sliding the robe out under the covers onto the floor.

'Better?' Hudson's voice was very deep and very dry.

She bit on her lips before managing, 'Yes, thank you.'

'Good. Get some sleep, Annie.'

Easier said than done, she thought irritably, gazing crossly into the shadows as dark outlines became faintly visible. No doubt he had slept with a member of the opposite sex more times than he could remember, but this was a first for her, and the circumstances couldn't have been more awful. She felt the hot sting of tears at the back of her eyes and spoke fiercely to herself. None of that, none of that; deep breaths and you'll go to sleep. But she had never felt less like sleep in her life.

Although the bed was vast, and the pile of pillows

made a successful barrier, Marianne was vitally aware of every tiny movement Hudson made in the next hour or so as she struggled to fall asleep. She tried to relax, willing her mind to empty and her limbs to loosen up, but it was torture to know the man she loved was inches away and wanting her—if only physically.

She had just decided that she was never going to get to sleep that night, and that she would give it another few minutes and then quietly slip out of bed and find herself a soft drink from the small fridge in the corner of the sitting room, when she awoke in the pale half-light of dawn. She'd gone to sleep! She lay for a moment, wondering what time it was, before carefully raising her arm to glance at her small silver wristwatch.

'It's five o'clock.' Hudson's voice was deep and soft at the side of her, and she froze for an instant, her eyes flicking to the heaped pillows, before she forced herself to speak.

'Is it?' she asked carefully.

'I know because I've watched every hour come and go,' he continued quietly, before raising himself on one elbow and peering over the downy barrier at her, his eyes soft and warm.

'You couldn't sleep?' It was a stupid question in view of what he'd just said, but the sight of him had taken all coherent thought clean away. His hair was ruffled slightly—the harsh hairstyle he favoured wouldn't allow more than slightly—and black stubble gave a sexiness to the square jaw that was dynamite.

'No, Annie, I couldn't sleep,' he said with rueful sarcasm.

'Oh, I'm sorry; you'll be tired later.' As sparkling repartee it failed miserably, but it was the best she could do in the circumstances, with every nerve she possessed in overdrive.

'Possibly.' His eyes moved over her, and she pulled the thin sheet up round her neck as discreetly as she could, a burning glow in the smoky grey eyes reminding her of her scanty attire. 'But I'll survive. On a difficult case I sometimes only catnap for the odd half an hour and work through the night for a week or more. It's amazing how you adjust when you have to.'

'That can't be good for you.' She was genuinely horrified.

He shrugged offhandedly. 'I've only myself to consider so it's not a problem, and I've never needed much sleep anyway.'

'No, but your health is important and—'

'I've always wondered what you look like in the morning when you first wake up, and now I know.'

The dark voice was husky and rich, and Marianne's senses exploded. She'd dreamt of waking up beside him too—many times.

'Like a rumpled golden kitten, all silky curls and great honey and green eyes,' he continued softly. 'I want to make you purr, Annie, do you know that? And I could…beautifully.'

She didn't doubt it for a minute, she thought feverishly.

'And you know it too.' She lowered her lids quickly but it was too late; he'd read her innermost desire. 'So what's holding you back?' he asked with silky determination.

Derision was her only escape and she took it. 'You'd like to believe that, wouldn't you?' she said cuttingly, wielding the weapon of disdain as best she could, considering she was fluid inside. 'The great Hudson de Sance, best lawyer, best lover… Is there anything you don't think you're the best at?' she asked with lethal sarcasm, feigning disgust as she turned on her side away from him, jerking the bedclothes more tightly round her shoulders.

'Stop it, Annie.' His voice was gentle, his touch tender as he reached over and turned her to face him, holding her still when she would have jerked away. 'You're playing a part, and not even very well. I've met too many real bitches in my work to doubt it.'

'I don't know what you mean,' she said desperately.

'You spoke my name in your sleep, not once but several times,' he continued evenly. 'What were you dreaming about, Annie?'

'Nothing.' The sensation of entrapment was so real she could taste it, her stomach shuddering and twisting as the cool grey eyes pierced hers, and although she struggled to let nothing of what she was feeling show in her eyes he read the hot panic and fear. And this time he was allowing her no evasion.

'You moaned it,' he whispered relentlessly. 'Breathed it out in little soft sighs—and I knew what you were dreaming. Do you know how I knew?'

'I don't care,' she muttered frantically.

'Because I recognised the longing, the desire, the need.' His grip was firm, preventing her from moving and increasing the feeling of being cornered. He watched his words sink in before he continued, 'I want you, Annie. Badly.'

She lay motionless, conscious of a tearing pain deep inside. There were probably hundreds, thousands of men she could have married and to whom her connection with undesirables like Michael wouldn't have meant a thing. But Hudson wasn't one of them. She could never marry a man like Hudson and expect him to take the consequences of having a wife with the sort of family ties she had. She...she was no good for him—bad news.

'I don't want you.' She forced the words out through numb lips. 'It...it wouldn't work.'

'Liar.' His voice was without enmity, almost expressionless. 'I can't get you out of my head, Annie—strange that, isn't it?' he said reflectively. 'It's like you're in my blood, my bones, and I don't like it. I'm a man who likes being in control, but you know that,' he said, with a self-deprecating grimace. 'I don't like the feeling of being vulnerable.'

'I...I don't make you vulnerable.' She was stunned by his revelation, and scared. She could just about take it when he was cold and arrogant, or charming and beguiling. Even the sensual, dark side of him was something she could recognise and fight against. But this exposure of his inner self was lethal.

It made her want to cover his face in kisses, to hold him close and tell him she cared more than he would ever know. It was...pure torture, she thought, trembling.

'Yes, you do.' He drew back slightly, his voice steady and his face shadowed. 'There is only one other person who has ever done that to me, and I worked through that one.'

One other person? He saw the blow register in her eyes but she couldn't have spoken; the pain was too sickening.

'It's not what you're thinking.' There was a peculiar look on his face now, but although she searched his eyes his expression was inscrutable. 'It wasn't a woman—at least not in the sense you assume.'

'Wasn't it?' She didn't believe him and it showed.

'No.' And then he sighed, frustratedly, as he said, 'Damn it, I've told you this much, I may as well tell you the rest. I've never talked about this before to anyone, but I don't want you to get the wrong idea. I've a feeling there are too many secrets between us as it is.'

'You needn't explain anything to me,' she said stiffly, her voice and face telling him just the opposite.

'It was my mother, Annie,' he said softly. 'She left my father, me, our home when I was almost six years old—just walked out one day and didn't come back.' He had let go of her now but she made no effort to move, her eyes on his face. 'She left to go and live with her lover, my father's brother,' he continued with a quiet, steady flatness that told her the memory was still caustic.

'Your uncle?' She stared at him, horrified.

'My uncle,' he confirmed softly, his eyes growing reflective as he looked back down the years to the devastation and confusion of a little six-year-old boy and desperate husband.

'He left my aunt and cousins to be with her. It was an…unusual twist to the eternal triangle and rocked the immediate family, as you can imagine; the repercussions were endless. First the patriarch of the clan—my mother's father from whom I got my name—ordered my mother home but she wouldn't listen. He was a harsh man, strong, and I don't think he had imagined she wouldn't do as she was told—even though she was a grown woman of twenty-seven. Apparently he tried everything—blackmail, threats, enticements—but she wouldn't budge. She had far more of him in her than he realised,' he added bitterly.

'After a few weeks it became apparent she wasn't coming back. She…she made no effort to contact us, so my grandfather made my father see her to ask for a reconciliation. She didn't want it. She told him she wanted a new life with Claude, that he was all that mattered to her.'

Marianne didn't dare ask what his mother had said about him, but in the next breath he told her, more by what he didn't say than what he did.

'She wanted all ties with her old life cut,' he said quietly. 'Severed clean. She made a deal with my grandfather after my father had seen her. In payment for her and Claude moving right away, to a different country where Claude had business contacts and where the scandal would be kept to a minimum, he would see that she was rewarded financially. My grandfather agreed.'

'But you told me when we first met that your parents had died when you were a child.' Marianne stared at his dark face. 'Didn't you?'

'They did.' He smiled mirthlessly, and again she knew he was feeling far more than he was revealing. How could his mother, how could any woman, walk out on a small boy and wash her hands of him so heartlessly? she asked herself bewilderedly, rage and pain and horror filling her heart. What must it have done to him, to his belief in family values, everything? And then she understood something she had never understood before.

That was part of what drove him, she thought wonderingly. His championship of the helpless, the victims, the abused and hurting, was all linked to the pain he had suffered when he had been small and helpless. That was why his work was so important to him, so vital. It wasn't just a quest for power and a brilliant career, it was part of his soul. It also explained the sheer ruthless control Hudson could bring to play on his feelings when necessary—he'd had a lifetime of practice.

'After a year of living in New Zealand my uncle decided he was having to work too hard at making a living,' Hudson continued cynically. 'My mother had used my grandfather's money to set Claude up in his own business, but it didn't go as well as he expected. So he left my mother and returned to his wife and family. My aunt was a Catholic and had refused to give him a divorce—she welcomed him back with open arms, so I understand. My mother…my mother killed herself when she knew he wasn't coming back,' he finished expressionlessly.

'Oh—oh, Hudson. No…' The pain was strangling her voice and constricting her breath.

'I couldn't understand why she would choose death when my father had asked her to come home to me and to him.' Hudson shook his head slowly, his voice a million miles away. 'Why oblivion was preferable to being my mother. I'd written to her, a little note along with my father's letter begging her to come home, and in it I told her how much I loved her, that I'd be a good boy if she came home, that she'd never have to tell me off again. It haunted me for a long time after she'd gone—the fact that I might have been naughty and caused her to go. I could be naughty in those days,' he added with an attempt at lightness as his eyes came back to the present and to Marianne.

'Of course I realise now there was far more going on than a small boy could understand, but at the time that was the only way I could see it. And no one *talked* to me, not really. My father was too devastated—he loved her desperately, you see—and my grandfather had ordered that her name must never be spoken—all the sorts of things you could possibly expect in a situation like that,' he added cryptically.

'Anyway, within a few months my father was dead too. The medical diagnosis was a bad heart, but I think he just stopped wanting to live when the knowledge that she was really gone hit him. Before she died he'd imagined, hoped, he might get her back one day.'

'And you? What happened to you?' Marianne asked softly.

'Me? I went to live with my grandfather and I trained myself not to think of my parents, not to want them, not to need them, and it worked...after a time,' he said grimly.

'And your uncle?'

'Claude only stayed with his wife a couple of years; I think the damage that had been done to the relationship was too great to overcome. My aunt didn't trust him any more, and she had good cause, as it happens, because he went off with his secretary whom he'd apparently been seeing even before he started the affair with my mother. Messy.' His mouth twisted. 'Very messy.'

'Hudson, I'm so sorry.' It was the wrong thing to say and she knew it immediately his expression changed.

'I'm not asking for sympathy, Annie; don't think that,' he said crisply. 'Emotional blackmail isn't my scene.'

'I know, I know that,' she said quickly, the ring of honesty in her voice causing the hardness to disappear.

'There are many people out there facing worse,' he said quietly. 'Who live behind a façade all their lives. I had the privilege of wealth to ease the way; some of them are destitute and utterly alone. But I can understand them, you see, get into their minds,' he said softly. 'I used to go on long walks as a child so I could be by myself; my grandfather was an overbearing guardian, and sometimes I needed a chance just to lie down somewhere and scream and cry and rage for my mother to come back, beg for a chance to see her just one more time, even though I knew it was impossible. People still hope for the impossible even when all chance of it has gone, and occasionally, just occasionally, I can make the impossible happen. The bad guys don't always have it their way.'

She didn't dare breathe in case he stopped the glimpse into his soul that she knew he had never shown anyone else.

'Nothing is black and white, Annie; the shades of grey are infinite,' he continued almost dreamily. 'We all have our own secret nightmares and hurts and mistakes, but someone, somewhere, has to *care* sometimes. Does that make sense?' he asked suddenly, the softness dying as he realised all he had revealed.

'Yes, yes, it does.' Her love for him was so intense it was causing a physical ache.

The agonising revelation about the misery of his childhood, his insight and sensitivity towards human nature and the needs and longings of ordinary folk was dangerous stuff, weakening her resolve and increasing her love and desire to fever pitch. She needed him—and as his head bent to take her lips she didn't resist.

She wanted to lose herself in him, tell him the truth and put the burden of decision on him. She was tired, so very, very tired of living in the world she inhabited, of never feeling real joy or real happiness, only occasionally watered-down facsimiles of the real thing. Without him the sky was greyer, the air heavier, life duller—beauty didn't touch her in the same way any more and she wanted to be the old Marianne, not this lifeless creature she saw in the mirror each morning.

As her lips opened beneath his she heard the little groan he gave, deep in his throat, at her capitulation, and then it was all pleasure and frenzied delight, her hands moving up to his shoulders and into the virile crispness of his hair as he leant over her.

She realised she was kissing him back with more abandon than she had ever shown, and that they were both shaking with the force of the burning waves of pleasure that were melting and moulding them to each other; her self-control had been discarded along with her reason. She loved him, she wanted him, she needed him...beyond that she couldn't think. Didn't *want* to think.

'Annie, Annie...' His lips trailed burning kisses over her face, her eyelids, her throat. 'You feel so good, so good...'

His hands and mouth were creating a fire that only his body could quench and she was molten in his arms, her blatant need stimulating his desire still more. Hudson was half kneeling on the bed now, his powerful frame bent over the ridge of pillows as she clung to his neck and his fingers deep in the tangled curls that had worked free of the plaits in the night.

'Say it; say you want me, Annie...' His voice was deep and husky and she obeyed it blindly, but she got the words wrong, speaking from the depths of her heart rather than her intellect.

'I love you, Hudson...' She was so lost in the enchantment, she was quite unaware of what she had revealed. 'I love you...'

Hudson raised his head, his eyes searching her abandoned face with its closed eyes, her eyelashes thick and dark on her flushed cheeks, before he said, 'Annie? Annie, look at me.'

She came back from the world of light and sensation slowly, and he gave her a little shake as he said again, 'Open your eyes; look at me. I want you fully *compos mentis*, damn it.'

'What...what is it?' She was trembling, her overwhelming need for him making her voice throaty and her eyes wild. 'What's wrong?' What had she done to make him look at her like that?

He had drawn back a little, his eyes examining her face feature by feature. 'You were a virgin when we first met,' he said softly. 'Why was that?'

'Why?' She stared at him as if he had gone mad. 'Because...because I'd never met anyone...' Her voice trailed away. What was this? What was wrong? 'I don't understand,' she whispered shakily. 'What has that got to do with...with now?'

'Anyone you loved?' he finished quietly, and now she knew there was something badly wrong. It was there in the darkly assessing power of his gaze, in the analytic scrutiny. Suddenly he was in lawyer mode, and it frightened her. 'Anyone you *loved*, Annie?'

'I suppose so,' she said warily, pulling herself into a sitting position with the sheet tight in her clenched fists against her breastbone. 'Why? Does it matter?'

'Yes, it matters.' He scanned her face with the laser eyes. 'And you're a virgin now, aren't you, Annie?' It was a statement, not a question, and she stared at him as her mind raced back and forth, a recollection—misty but becoming more substantial—causing her to freeze.

She hadn't said those words, had she? That faint echo that was reverberating in her head? She couldn't have...

'In the last two years you have seen no one, had no relationship of a personal nature at all. There have been those who tried—several—but you didn't want to know.' His voice *sounded* like a lawyer's now, his brain almost visibly putting two and two together and making... Making a number that spelled trouble.

'How do you know?' She forced antagonism into the gap between her and disaster. 'I could have—'

'Marjorie.' His voice was relentless. 'Marjorie told me.'

'Oh, Marjorie!' She tried for a dismissive laugh, her voice derisive. 'You mean to say you listened to Marjorie?'

'Yes, Marjorie. Who had no axe to grind, no reason to lie, who is in fact a gossip of the first order and would have been sure to repeat any tasty little titbit if there had been one. In fact you puzzled her; I could tell. She didn't know whether to admire you or feel sorry for you—'

'I don't need anyone to feel sorry for me,' she bit back quickly, stung to the core. 'I manage perfectly well, thank you.'

'We all need the warmth of human compassion at times, Annie,' Hudson said grimly. 'However much we try to hide the fact.'

'And that's what you think I'm doing? Hiding the fact?' She prevaricated swiftly. 'You've no right to assume that.'

He didn't fall for the decoy ploy, going straight for the jugular instead. 'You said you loved me, just now, when you weren't thinking ten steps in advance.' The grey eyes had the consistency of liquid steel. 'You told me you loved me two years ago, and I believed it then too. I *know* it was the truth, here, where it counts.' He touched his chest, his eyes intent on her face.

'Hudson—'

'So if you loved me then and you love me now, and there's been no high life, no parties, no lovers...' He paused, his eyes searching her face, which was the colour of lint. 'And no elusive fiancé either...' he stated slowly, each word a revelation. 'There *wasn't* a man, was there, Annie? *Hell, what a fool I've been.* I wondered why I couldn't find him, why no one you'd been at college with had the faintest idea what I was talking about.'

'You didn't see my college friends?' She stared at him, horrified. 'You had no right to do that.'

'I had all the right in the world both then and now,' he growled softly. 'You love me. I should have listened to my heart.'

'No, you're wrong; everyone says that when they're...they're...'

She went to twist out of the bed but his voice stopped her before she had barely moved. 'Stay still; stay right where you are, Annie, or so help me I won't be responsible for my actions.'

'Are you threatening me?' she asked tightly.

'Whatever it takes, sweetheart, whatever it takes.'

'This is crazy, Hudson,' she whispered faintly. 'Let me go.'

'No, it's me that's been crazy,' he said slowly. 'What a fool, what an incredibly blind fool I've been. I should have known you aren't capable of betraying me like that, but I let myself be persuaded. Me, of all people. Hell, I make my living going on gut instinct and fact, and I had neither in your case—merely words and more words. And the words didn't make sense even then.'

'They did; you're just determined to make a mystery out of this.'

'That night two years ago, when you agreed to marry me, you were happy—really happy. There was nothing, not a hint of anything being wrong. I should know— I've dissected that time often enough,' he added bitterly. 'And then, within hours, it'd all changed. What happened when you left me that night, Annie?' he asked softly. 'Because sure as hell something did. Something…catastrophic.' His eyes were boring into her soul.

This was too close—he was getting too close.

'And whatever it was it didn't stop you loving me.' There was a thread of something in the tightly controlled voice—joy? Relief?—that told her she had to finish this before it went any further. 'You loved me then and you love me now. Say it?'

She opened her mouth to tell him she didn't love him, that he was wrong, quite, quite wrong in his arrogant assumptions, but she couldn't do it. She might have been able to bluff her way if his own tragic truth about his childhood hadn't seared her heart so badly, or if the picture of a bewildered child, with eyes the colour of stormy seas, wasn't etched indelibly on the screen of her mind, but as it was she just couldn't lie again. And so she stared at him, her mouth half-open and her eyes panic-stricken.

'Annie?' He touched her face tenderly. 'I'm not your enemy.'

It was the gentleness that did it, that made her realise she couldn't live with herself—let alone him—if she were the tool used to sully his reputation and destroy his credibility.

'I don't want a relationship with you, Hudson, now or ever. And I want to go back to Tangier now, today,' she said shakily.

'You haven't answered my question, Annie,' he said evenly.

'I just did.' She forced her eyes not to flinch from his.

'No, that was like everything else you've said since the day we met again—garbage!' The words shot out like bullets, and she shrank back against the bedhead, shocked by the sudden change in him. But she shouldn't have been; she should have been expecting it, she thought in the next instant. He was using every trick he'd learnt since he'd first stepped into a courtroom, and he was good—he was very, very good at what he did. It stiffened her resolve in a way that would have made him kick himself if he'd known.

'Garbage maybe, fact definitely,' she said shortly.

'I can stay here as long as it takes, Annie,' he warned softly.

'You are the last man, the very last man in all the world I would get involved with, Hudson.'

It had the unmistakable ring of truth to it, and she saw the words register in his eyes as his face went white.

They sat for a full minute in a silence that was electric before he said, his voice toneless, 'You aren't denying you love me but you're saying you want nothing to do with me. Right?'

'Yes.' The one word said it all; she did not need to elaborate.

She stared down at her hands, tightly clasped together on the sheet, and swallowed painfully. This was terrible, worse than she ever could have imagined. And it was all her fault.

'Yes.' He repeated the word grimly, but as she glanced up at him again his face was blank, devoid of emotion. 'And you expect me to accept that?' he said slowly. 'After all we meant to each other, the plans we made, you really think I would be content to let you go back to your new life without any explanation?'

What could she say? She stared at him wide-eyed until she couldn't bear to look at him any longer, and dropped her gaze to her hands again, her nerves twisted and taut. 'You have no choice,' she stated as firmly as she could, considering her heart was thundering in her ears so loudly it was deafening. 'It's what I want.'

'And what about what *I* want?' he bit back angrily. 'Don't you think that comes into the equation at all? You don't think you're perhaps being a teeny bit selfish, Annie?' The last carried such icy sarcasm that she felt herself shrivel up and die. 'I have needs, emotions too; I'm not made of stone, damn it.'

'Yes, I know.' She desperately tried to keep all trace of the pain that was tearing her apart from showing. 'And I'm sorry.'

'Oh, sure,' he bit out savagely. 'I can see that.'

'But I have to be true to myself, to what I want,' she carried on, trembling. 'I want to have a career, to make my mark, and I couldn't do that if I was involved with…with anyone. That's why I decided not to date in London; I want to put all my energy and time into my work. Some women might be able to divide themselves in half a dozen different directions, but I'm not like that, and I know…I know what I want.'

'And to hell with the rest of the world?' He twisted away from her, moving to his side of the bed with his back to her as he raked his hands through his hair.

'If…if you like,' she said numbly.

'Funnily enough I don't like at all,' he said icily. 'You look so soft and sweet, Annie. How can that gentle exterior hide such ruthless purpose?'

'It's the way I am.' Would he believe her? He had to.

'So you are saying you would sacrifice anything we might have together without allowing me any opinion of my own?' he said grimly. 'You won't discuss why you left me two years ago and why you won't stay now? Right?'

'Yes.' Her fists were pressed into the hollow between her breasts, the pain in her heart so excruciating it was stopping her breath.

'To hell with it.' He stood up and walked into the bathroom, slamming the door violently behind him.

CHAPTER EIGHT

THANKS to a wealthy friend of Hassan's who was pleased to put his private plane at their disposal, Marianne and Hudson were back in Tangier by early afternoon.

Marianne was in agony, silent, excruciating agony that was made all the worse by having to maintain a cool, calm outward façade for the world in general and Hudson in particular. She talked, she ate, she drank, she moved her arms and legs, and had even managed the odd smile and spot of cheerful repartee when they'd taken their leave of Hassan and his family, but inside she was bleeding and raw and without hope.

She didn't know how Hudson was feeling. Earlier that morning, when he had emerged from the bathroom clean-shaven and showered, she had immediately scuttled in with her clothes and make-up and hadn't emerged until she was groomed and ready to face him.

She had expected... She hadn't really known what she expected, she reflected now as a taxi took them back to their original hotel where they had left most of their belongings, but it hadn't been this coldly pleasant, inscrutable stranger at the side of her. He had been cool and helpful when he had suggested he telephone the airport in Tangier and arrange a flight home to London for her before they had left Hassan's home, solicitous for her comfort during the journey—if remote—and calm and agreeable to the change of their plans at all times, and yet... She didn't have a clue as to how he was really feeling. The mask he wore so often in his chosen profession was very firmly in place.

'May I have your address in London?' His voice was

courteous and distant—the sort of voice one used when asking something which was expected by the other party, but not particularly desired by the one asking.

And its very remoteness enabled Marianne to say, with an aplomb she was amazed at, 'I don't think so.'

'As you will.' The taxi came to a halt outside the hotel as he spoke, and as Marianne stepped into the dull, hot, sluggish air she felt a sudden and violent longing for the inclement cool weather she had left behind in England. It had been hot in France when she had first met Hudson an eternity ago, and it was hot now. Suddenly the rain and fog of England took on a poignancy that was painful—spelling out refuge to her exhausted, weary mind.

'Your flight is at six this evening and it's...' he consulted the heavy gold watch on his wrist '...almost two now. Would you like me to arrange for a light meal to be served once you've freshened up?'

''No, no, it's perfectly all right; I'm not hungry,' she said quickly. She couldn't have put into words what his cold courtesy was doing to her, but she knew if she didn't separate herself from him soon she would do or say something she'd regret for the rest of her life. 'I... Thank you very much for the trip.' She stuck out a small hand for him to shake, her face as white as a sheet and her back straight. 'It was very good of you.'

'Good of me?' He took her arm, his fingers absently massaging her wrist as his hand slid down her silky flesh. 'I don't think so,' he said softly as he walked her into Reception. 'Self-indulgent maybe, manipulative even, but not good.'

She missed her step as her head shot up to see his face, but it was quite expressionless. 'Hudson—'

'Your taxi will be here within the hour,' he continued evenly. 'So if you would like to use my room in the meantime I'll wait in the coffee lounge. Goodbye, Annie.'

'Goodbye?' Suddenly the moment of separation was here and she couldn't handle it. 'But... Aren't you going to be around? The key…' She looked down at his room key which he had placed in her fingers moments before.

'Leave it with Reception.' He bent forward, kissing her lightly and coolly on the forehead, before straightening and smiling as he said, 'Perhaps we'll meet again in another two years; who knows?'

And then he turned, walking away quickly and decisively without a backward glance and taking her heart with him.

Marianne showered and changed in the impersonal luxury of Hudson's suite, spending long minutes with her head uplifted to the cool, silky flow of water which erased the burning effect of her hot, salty tears, and was back down in Reception in time for the taxi which arrived promptly at three.

The tears had alleviated none of the grinding misery that was gripping her throat in a stranglehold, merely increasing the thumping pressure of the headache she had had since first thing that morning. She looked for Hudson in Reception—she couldn't help it—but there was no tall, dark, forbidding man with eyes the colour of stone, just the pretty little receptionist and smiling, pock-marked taxi driver who had already loaded her suitcases into his vehicle. Hudson had finally washed his hands of her—it was over.

She wanted to cry all the way to the airport but she didn't, gazing out of the grimy taxi window at the bright, sun-drenched changing view beyond, and wondering how on earth she was going to get through the rest of the day—let alone the rest of her life.

And then, as she stepped into the terminal, he was there in front of her, his grey eyes meeting hers calmly. 'Hudson?' For a second her defences were down and he read everything she felt in her unguarded gaze, before the shutters slammed into place. 'What are you doing here?' She took a deep breath but it was no good; her voice didn't belong to her. 'We…we said goodbye.'

'I need to talk to you.' He took the cases from her unresisting hands before she had time to pull herself together, marching her over to a quiet corner and sitting her down on a hard plastic bench. 'And I want you to listen to me.'

'I've got to check in—'

'You've plenty of time.' He cut through her shaky protest too quickly, his abruptness revealing he wasn't as cool as he appeared. 'It won't take long.'

'But I thought... You said at the hotel...' And then she understood. A tactic. Another tactic. He was using everything he had ever learnt to wear her down, and it had nearly succeeded. She hadn't been able to believe the blinding sense of joy when she had seen his face after thinking she would never see him again, and he had *planned* it, used his knowledge of human weakness, manipulated her again as he'd confessed he'd done before. But somehow, as she met his level gaze, she couldn't be angry. He loved her. It was there in his face. And he was fighting in the only way he knew how— ruthlessly. He would never know how she wished he could succeed.

'You don't want to hear this but I'm going to say it anyway,' he said flatly. 'Even though I'm probably making a fool of myself for the second time in my life. I don't understand why you left me before and I don't understand why you're leaving me now, but I have never stopped loving you for one hour, one minute, one second.'

He took a deep breath, his eyes wretched. 'Now, I thought at one time you didn't care, that it had all been a lie, but I don't think that now. You care, damn it.'

'Hudson, this will do no good for either of us.' She went to rise but he wouldn't let her, his hands shooting out to take her arms, his grip bruising.

'Oh, yes, it will, for me at least,' he said grimly. 'There has never been anyone else but you, Annie. Oh, I've had other relationships in the past, some good and

some not so good, but none of them touched the core of
me. I couldn't believe—' He stopped abruptly, taking a
shuddering breath before he continued, 'I couldn't believe how you made me feel, in here.' He touched his
chest softly. 'Like a kid again, a young boy. I wanted
to shout and brag and do ridiculous things to impress
you—me, Hudson de Sance, cynical and worldly-wise
sceptic that I was. And then you left.' He shook his head
slowly, his eyes stormy.

'I told you, in the letter,' she whispered tremulously,
the shaking deep inside her stomach so bad it was making her nauseous. 'I couldn't fit in with what you
wanted—'

He swore, softly but with an intentness that shocked
her, before he said, 'No more lies, Annie. If you can't
tell me the truth say nothing at all, but no more lies. I
don't know what happened that night you promised to
marry me, but, whether it was demons from the past or
something that occurred then, we can fight it together if
you let me in. Damn it, you're not happy, I'm not
happy—what have you got to lose?' he asked urgently.

Me? Nothing. You—everything you've worked for all
your life. But she couldn't say it.

'You'll find someone else.' She stared at him, her eyes
huge. 'Like...like Jasmine.' It was unreasonable, wickedly unreasonable, in the circumstances, but the redhead's presence in his life still had the power to unnerve
her.

'Jasmine?' He shook his head slowly. 'Annie, Jasmine
is the wife of Idris's cousin, and even if she wasn't I
wouldn't touch her with a bargepole. The relationship
is, as they say, purely platonic.' He eyed her soberly. 'I
came to Morocco to see you and you only after I discovered your whereabouts. There was no business trip
or planned holiday; I just dropped everything and got
my tail out here.'

'No...' It was the last thing she'd expected.

'Yes.' His mouth twisted in a wry smile. 'And it'd

help if you looked less horrified. I love you, Annie, and I want you in my bed, my home, my life, my soul, but not for a month or a year. I want to marry you, and this is the last time of asking. Whatever you say now, I shan't ask again. I'll be there for you, I'll take anything you can give and make it work, whatever's happened in the past, but I don't intend to keep on asking. I love you, and I know, whatever you say and whatever you've done, that you love me. I don't understand you but I love you. Well?'

He paused, his eyes dark with emotion and his mouth taut. 'What's it to be?' he asked quietly. 'A future together or goodbye?'

She stared at him, the colour coming and going in her face and the faintness in her head making her dizzy. Oh, Hudson, she thought, I love you so much. Please try to understand, my love. You will meet someone else; there are hundreds of women out there who would give everything they possess to be your wife, so there's got to be someone you could love in return. But it can't be me. Not if you want it all. With me it's a choice, and if I made you make that choice, forced you to give up everything you love, you'd begin to hate me. Perhaps in a year, maybe five, but eventually...

'Goodbye, Hudson.' She stood up slowly, and this time he made no effort to restrain her as she reached for her bags. 'You might not believe this right now but I want you to be happy,' she said tonelessly, forcing all emotion out of her voice as she said what she had to say. 'And I know you wouldn't be with me, whatever you think.' There was an unnerving silence while she waited for him to speak, but he said nothing, his eyes unreadable as they searched her pale face in which all vestige of colour was gone, and he still said nothing as she walked out of sight.

The next two or three weeks were the sort of nightmare Marianne wouldn't have wished on her worst enemy.

She returned from Morocco utterly worn out and emotionally drained, her anguish increasing rather than lessening as time went on.

She worked all hours of the day and night, but still found it difficult to sleep despite a grinding exhaustion that showed in a dramatic loss of weight and deep blue-mauve shadows under her eyes. But she resisted sleeping pills—they wouldn't help what ailed her. She knew Keith and the others were worried about her, one or two friends even taking it upon themselves to call round to her flat and gently enquire as to what was wrong, but her pain and confusion were too deep to discuss. She felt bereft, without hope, and the future stretched ahead like a great black chasm in which there was nothing but despair and a terrifying loneliness.

It was in the middle of her third week back in London, when she had struggled to work on a rainy, cold morning that resembled October rather than late June, that Keith called her into his office, his voice excited and shrill.

'What do you know about an organisation called Major Promotions?' he asked before she had even got through the door. 'They're based in the States but have subsidiaries in Canada and Australia. Have you ever worked for them in the past?'

'Major Promotions?' She tried to force a vestige of interest and intelligence into her voice. 'I don't think...'

'Think, Marianne, think.' Keith was all but dancing. 'A name, someone you've met at a shoot or perhaps socially, a friend of a friend? You must know someone connected with them?'

'I'm sorry, Keith, but Major Promotions does nothing for me,' Marianne said quietly. 'Is there any reason why it should?'

'Well, they certainly know you.' Keith waved her to be seated, his voice gleeful. 'Or *of* you at least. And what they know they like. I got a letter this morning. Here, read that.'

He flung a piece of paper across to her and she saw

it was a letter on beautifully embossed thick notepaper of the finest quality.

'They're interested in us, or rather you, covering a project they're doing with some of the top names in advertising in the States,' Keith continued before she had had time to read a word. 'It's all on conservation, but just read some of the names who are involved with it—go on, read them—'

'Keith, give me a minute, would you?' Enough was enough—she couldn't think straight with him chirping on like that.

'Oh, yeah, right, sorry. Read on.' He sat back and waited.

It was quite clear-cut. They wanted Marianne Harding and they were prepared to pay for the privilege—from the generous offer outlined in the document in front of her it appeared money was no object. And the project was indeed a mind-blowing one, as were the celebrity names connected with it. What it didn't say—Marianne's brow wrinkled—was how they had heard of her in the first place. Keith she could have understood, but Marianne Harding? Who was Marianne Harding to these sorts of people? She asked Keith the same question, her voice perplexed.

'I thought you'd be the one to tell *me* that.' He stared at her puzzled face. 'You mean you really don't know where the link is?' he asked after a few seconds had ticked by.

'Not a clue.' She had been racking her brains to no avail.

'Oh, what does it matter anyway?' Keith said briskly. 'The point is they've heard of you and they want you, and that can only spell opportunity to you and the business. They want you to fly over at the end of the month—that's not a problem, is it? I've got to fax them with our acceptance and then set the ball rolling.'

'But...but do you think I'm up to it?' Marianne asked

anxiously as her stomach began to turn over. 'It sounds like a massive project.' She glanced at the letter again.

'Of which you will be merely a tiny cog,' Keith said reassuringly. 'I've worked on things like this, Marianne; you won't be the only photographer, believe me. They often have several different things going at the same time and they always cover themselves for unforeseen difficulties. There'll be back-up, not that you'll need it,' he added encouragingly. 'It'll be a great experience for you.'

She nodded slowly. A few months, even a few weeks ago an opportunity like this one would have had her delirious with excitement, so why couldn't she feel even a tiny grain of enthusiasm now? she asked herself irritably. Why didn't it *matter*—even a little bit? But it didn't. She felt apprehensive that she might not be up to scratch, but beyond that—nothing.

Oh... She physically shook her head, disgusted at herself. She couldn't go on like this. She had to pull herself together, look to her career and her future—it was all she was ever going to have, after all. That thought did nothing to lessen the black cloud that was permanently in place these days.

'So...I'll fax them, shall I?' Keith sounded put out.

It was clear Keith couldn't understand her lack of enthusiasm, and she really couldn't blame him, Marianne thought miserably. She didn't understand it, or herself, either. Somehow it was as if the lights had been turned off deep inside—everything was dark and shadowy and pointless—and it scared her, because even in the worst days during the time after she had first left Hudson two years ago she hadn't felt quite like this.

But she would get through. She set her teeth and listened to Keith enthusing on. It was either that or give in, and she was a fighter—the last two years had taught her that. If she gave in then Michael and the evil men who were still alive and perpetuating their poison would have won on every count, and that wasn't to be borne. She just wished she knew Hudson was all right.

She was telling herself exactly the same thing five days later as a cab raced her through the teeming streets of New York. Even in her misery the pace and vibrant life of the famous metropolis was thrilling, its mass of human inhabitants scurrying about the sidewalks like tiny ants with the huge towering buildings seeming more suited to an advanced computer game than real life. And she was part of it…for a while.

She was glad the job hadn't been in Washington DC, where Hudson lived and worked. For all its wonderful potential and future possibilities she would have had to turn it down, ridiculous though it would have seemed to Keith and everyone else. But the slightest, the merest chance of meeting Hudson would have meant she couldn't accept it. She couldn't live through another meeting with him and emerge sane.

The cab stopped in front of a building that was identical to the ones surrounding it, but none the less impressive because of it. She stood looking up at the myriad windows for some moments after she had paid the driver, the warm June breeze teasing the few tendrils of hair that had escaped the businesslike knot on top of her head and stroking her cheeks softly.

It was hot, very hot—an unexpected heatwave, the cab driver had said—but she felt quite comfortable in a smart white linen suit, its short skirt and tailored jacket both feminine and chic. She hadn't been too sure about the white high-heeled court shoes—she had always had a fear of sprawling at someone's feet when she wore heels over an inch high for work—but the Italian shoes had gone so beautifully with the suit, she hadn't been able to resist wearing them, knowing they gave an elegance to the outfit that was striking. And she felt she needed to look her best.

This meeting was merely a chat to cover any loose ends regarding the job anyway, she reassured herself as she stepped through massive doors into the building, which was all air-conditioning and ankle-deep carpeting. She'd be sitting down for most of it, no doubt.

She gave her name at Reception as instructed, and immediately a tall, fair-haired man who had been standing to one side of the reception desk sprang to her side. 'Miss Harding?' He seemed faintly familiar but she couldn't work out why. 'They're expecting you upstairs, in the Blue Suite. Please allow me to escort you there. My name is Bill Truscott by the way,' he added smilingly.

'Thank you.' She stared at him in surprise. She was just a very minor little cog in the grand clock that made up Major Promotions——Keith had told her that more than once over the last few days, as much to reassure her that the success of the whole project wasn't hanging on her camera as to satisfy a little grain of personal pique that it hadn't been *his* services Major Promotions had asked for——and she certainly hadn't expected to be met in Reception by anyone. Perhaps that was a courtesy they extended to everyone she thought to herself as she followed Bill Truscott to the lifts. Americans were always very sociable and genial, after all. That must be it.

The lift was mirrored and carpeted, and as it took them swiftly upwards she forced herself to ask, 'Has…has everyone else arrived, Mr Truscott?' She was feeling nervous now, and the only way to combat it was to talk normally.

'Pretty much——and the name's Bill.' He smiled again, and the strange feeling that had assailed her before was back, but more strongly. She found herself staring at him for a moment, and quickly lowered her gaze when a pair of smoky grey eyes registered her regard. Goodness, he'd think she fancied him at this rate.

'Good flight?' He was far more at ease than she was. 'I understand you arrived yesterday; I hope you've recovered from the jet-lag a little now?' he added politely.

'Yes, thank you.' She met his gaze again and forced

her expression into neutral. 'The hotel is lovely and the room is very comfortable.' In truth she had slept better the night before than in weeks, much to her surprise, although it had still taken careful application of make-up to hide the shadows under her eyes.

'Good, good.' The lift slid to a halt and they stepped into a corridor beautifully decorated in muted shades of blue. 'The suite is just along here, if you'd like to follow me.'

She suddenly recognised that the unease she was feeling was more than just mere nerves at the forthcoming meeting, but she couldn't pin down the reason for the icy little trickles flickering down her backbone. But they were there.

'Mr Truscott—Bill?' She caught his arm as they made their way towards a door at the very end of the corridor. 'Could I just ask you something?' she said quickly.

'Of course; ask away.' He smiled, but there was a reserve, a faint wariness that made her stammer as she said, 'Do...do I know you? I mean, have...have we met before?'

'I don't think so.' They were at the door now and he paused, his voice soft as he added, 'Don't look so scared, Annie; no one is going to eat you.'

'Annie?' The name hit her like a thunderbolt but in the next instant he opened the door and pushed her gently inside, straight into Hudson's waiting arms.

CHAPTER NINE

'HUDSON?' Marianne just had time to breathe his name, her eyes opening into wide green pools, before his mouth closed over hers in a kiss that was fierce and hard and had the hunger of years in it. She couldn't do a single thing to resist him, her mind stunned and disbelieving even as her senses soared and spun until she thought she would faint. He was here. He was here...

As always fire exploded between them the second their mouths fused, and as he moulded her possessively into his hard male frame she clung to him, unable to believe it was really happening.

The door had shut quietly behind them once Marianne was inside the room but neither of them was aware of it, their minds and souls and bodies wrapped in each other to the point where nothing and no one else existed.

It was as Hudson groaned and crushed her further into him that he seemed to gain control of himself, his mouth lifting from hers as he took a long, deep pull of air, his breathing ragged.

'I don't understand...' If it hadn't been for his strong arms holding her she would have fallen to the floor, her legs useless. 'What... Where is everyone? The meeting...'

'There is no meeting—or, to be precise, there is one, but next week, and either you or Keith can attend.'

His voice was shaking but she was too stunned herself to notice. 'It's not now? But...that man.' She glanced round wildly for Bill Truscott. 'He was going to take me there.'

'He's waiting in the adjoining room, along with other relatives and friends,' Hudson said softly. 'Admittedly not yours—I couldn't risk someone telling you—but we can have another ceremony later if you want.' He was keeping tight hold of her.

'Who is he?' She could only focus on the man; the rest of this was too surreal. 'He...he looked familiar.'

'My cousin...and my best man.' The last was said softly and deeply, and accompanied by a tightening of his arms around her as his eyes devoured her confused, stricken face.

'Your best man? But...' She stared up at him, her face as white as the clothes she was wearing. 'You told me you weren't married,' she murmured faintly. 'Who...? When did you...?'

'I'm not, not yet,' Hudson said quietly. 'But I intend to be—very soon. And to you.'

'Me?' There was a distinct buzzing in her ears and she just managed to say, 'I think I need a glass of water or something,' before the room began to swim and dip and her legs folded.

He whisked her up in his arms immediately, carrying her over to a small sofa and giving her a glass of what looked very much like brandy once he had placed her on the cushioned seat. 'Drink it all,' he ordered softly, 'straight down. Bill had the foresight to think you might need it. Part of a best man's duties.'

She drank it straight down in spite of the fact she didn't care for brandy, and once the neat alcohol had burnt its way into her system the faintness receded, and as it disappeared reality dawned. 'Hudson?' She opened her eyes from where she had been lying back against the cushions to find him kneeling in front of her, his eyes on a level with hers. 'If this means what I think it means you're crazy, do you know that? I can't possibly—'

'I'm not going to ask you to marry me; the time for asking is finished with,' he said quietly, but with an intentness that was unnerving. 'I've tried the reasonable approach—hell, I've tried every damn thing—so now I'm going to make you marry me. I love you, Annie, and I know you love me. I've been in touch with some of your friends and they say you've been miserable, desperately miserable, since you came back from Morocco. And you're killing me,' he finished softly.

It wasn't happening; she'd finally flipped, she thought vacantly.

'So now I'm taking the initiative for a change.'

For a change? The ridiculousness of that statement would have brought a smile in any other circumstances.

'I'm not going to ask you what happened in France two years ago, or why you refused me again in Morocco—not now, not ever, Annie,' he continued steadily. 'I don't care what's stopped you being with me, only in so far as how it affects you, but whatever it is, however terrible, I'm not going to let it ruin both our lives. You love me enough for marriage—it was there in your eyes at the airport and it's there now. If there's one thing my work has taught me it's to forget about words and read the inner soul.' His voice was quiet but terrifyingly firm.

'No, I can't; you don't understand—'

'No, I don't,' he agreed quietly. 'Perhaps I never will, but that's up to you. Through that door—' he pointed to the inter-connecting door and her eyes followed his hand '—are some of my relations and closest friends waiting to see a minister perform a wedding ceremony for us. Apart from Bill no one knows the circumstances and what it's taken to get you here, so if you let me down now—if you walk away—you'll be making me look a fool in front of everyone who matters to me. I'm not going to carry you kicking and screaming into that room.'

He paused, his heart in his eyes as he took in her white face and trembling lips. 'The choice is yours, Annie. But I want you and I intend to have you, and you want me—I know it. Whether it's now, a year from now, ten years from now, I shan't give up. And once we are married it will be all right; I promise you that.'

She had never wanted to believe in his confident assurance of his own power and authority so much, but, knowing what she did, it was impossible. 'And if it's not?' she whispered brokenly.

'It will be.' His eyes were intent on hers, the air vibrating with emotion. 'I've never broken a promise yet.'

'But if it's not?' she repeated tremulously. 'What then?'

'If after we're married you feel it's not working, I wouldn't hold you against your will,' he said evenly. 'Will that do?'

'You mean that?' Marianne searched his face helplessly.

'You have my word on it.'

A deadly silence followed his promise. Marianne's mind was racing, spinning, her face lint-white with two spots of burning colour staining her cheekbones. He had gambled everything on his belief that she loved him, and she did, she did so much. He wasn't wrong, and he knew he wasn't wrong. She should never have let him know and then this wouldn't have happened. She stared at him, seeing the love and desire in his dear face.

She was trapped. If she refused him now it would mean humiliation of the worst kind in front of everyone he cared for—if she went through with the ceremony she would become the match that could light the fire which would consume his career, his good name, everything he stood for. Michael's business partners might never contact her, might never follow through—but the risk was too high. *What should she do?*

And then, like a little gleam of light at the end of a dark tunnel, it came to her. If she went through with the marriage as Marianne *Harding* Michael's colleagues might not recognise her for who she really was, certainly for a while. And before they had time to put two and two together, even perhaps before the marriage became public knowledge, she could leave. He had promised her she could; he'd *promised*. It was all her fuddled brain could think of. 'What about all the documentation?' she asked shakily. 'You can't just get married at the drop of a hat—'

'All taken care of,' he said quickly. 'I am a lawyer, remember.'

'And my name?' She took a deep breath but her voice was still trembling so much, she could hardly get the words out. 'I want to be called Harding,' she said. 'It must be Harding.'

'The certificate might say something else, but in all other respects it will be Harding if that's what you want. Marianne Harding marrying Hudson de Sance—yes?' His eyes became more darkly intent. 'Why does the name matter, Annie?' he asked softly.

'You said...you said you wouldn't ask me any more questions.' It wasn't fair, but then this wasn't fair either, she thought numbly. And she couldn't think, couldn't decide what was best to do.

'So I did.' He stopped talking, staring at her with smoky grey eyes she could drown in. 'Decision time, then.'

'Hudson, this isn't right.' She tried one more time, but it was useless and she knew it. 'You must see that?'

'No, Annie, I don't. Besides which—' He stopped, a small smile twisting his mouth before he continued, 'You're even dressed for a wedding.' He indicated her white suit with a wave of his hand.

'Yes, I suppose I am.' It was the only way out, and as long as she left Hudson before her real identity became known it wouldn't harm him. *It must not.* But how would she be able to do that?

'And that means?' He was speaking quietly, steadily, but the little tremor in his voice that he couldn't quite hide caught at her heartstrings. He didn't know if she was going to walk away and leave him to explain away this whole fiasco. As if she could. *As if she could.* He had gambled everything on believing in her—she had to go through with it. *That was her answer.*

'I'll marry you, Hudson.' She spoke woodenly and he knew better than to push her any further, merely nodding soberly and getting to his feet as he gave her his hand and helped her rise.

She was a beautiful bride. Everyone said so. Before they had joined the others Hudson had taken the pins out of her hair, his touch tender and gentle, arranging the glowing golden mass across her shoulders before fixing a delicate band of tiny fresh white and pink rosebuds across the silky curls, the colours reflected in the lavish bouquet he placed into her numb fingers.

It wasn't just her fingers that were numb—she felt frozen all over, stupefied, her mouth repeating the necessary phrases during the service, and afterwards too when receiving the congratulations from the forty or so guests who had been gathered in the huge, beautifully decorated room beyond the one where she had met Hudson.

She said all the right things, smiled, nodded graciously, but inside she was dead, paralysed with shock and an overwhelming fear that she had just let Hudson make the worst mistake of his life.

'There's a wedding luncheon to get through and then we can slip away to the hotel,' Hudson whispered in her ear as he took her arm to leave. 'I've booked the bridal suite in the hotel in which you are staying—your things will have already been moved there.'

'You were very sure of me.' She wasn't angry; the ice round her emotions wouldn't let her be.

'No, no, I wasn't.' An inflexion in his voice, a rawness, made her glance up at him sharply, and she caught agony in his eyes before a veil blanketed his expression. 'I was sure you loved me, but beyond that...' His mouth twisted in the semblance of a smile. 'Beyond that I was sure of nothing.'

'And you still went through with it,' she whispered shakily.

'I had no other option.' He shook his head slowly. 'I'd tried everything else. But if later you want a ceremony in church with all the trimmings—white dress, bridesmaids and so on—'

'I had the white dress—suit,' she corrected numbly. 'And the clothes don't mean anything, do they?'

'No, Annie, the clothes mean nothing at all,' he agreed evenly.

The marriage luncheon stretched on into late afternoon, the beautiful June weather New York was enjoying meaning the guests spilled out into a pretty little courtyard attached to the excellent restaurant where Hudson had arranged the wedding meal.

Champagne flowed like water and Marianne had several glassfuls but very little food, the effervescent liquid providing the shot in the arm she needed to get through the day without breaking down, or allowing herself to surface from the dull stupor her senses had taken refuge in. It was as though it were happening to someone else.

There was the odd moment—for instance when she caught herself glancing at the wide gold wedding band on the third finger of her left hand, its presence alien and strange, or when someone jokingly addressed her as Mrs de Sance—when her poise faltered and a dart of feeling burnt its way through the ice, but on the whole the numbness prevailed, and Marianne welcomed it. The luxury of feeling would come later—for now she was on view and had to act the part allotted to her. She couldn't—wouldn't—let Hudson down in front of everyone.

It was as they prepared to leave the luncheon that the ice began to melt, when she discovered Hudson had arranged for a party of professional bell-ringers to come and play one of her favourite pieces by Handel. 'I couldn't have the church bells ringing,' he whispered in her ear as they listened to the music, 'so these wedding bells are the next best thing.'

'They're beautiful,' Marianne said quietly, the burden on her increasing a hundred-fold. If only he had been rough or cruel or thoughtless this would have been so much easier. But then she wouldn't have loved him, she reminded herself bleakly, and none of it would have happened anyway. He was everything she could ever have wanted in a husband. *Husband.* The word hit her like a ten-ton truck. He was her husband...they had got married. What had she done? *What had she done?* What would happen when the wedding bells stopped and they were alone, as man and wife?

Once the thaw started Marianne found it impossible to stop the melting effect on her emotions. They left the restaurant amid a deluge of confetti and good wishes, Hudson enigmatic and cool in his dark morning suit and snowy-white shirt, and once inside the wedding car—a huge, great sedan covered in white ribbons—she found she was shaking uncontrollably.

'It's all right, darling, it's all right.' Hudson drew her close as the car purred through the crowded busy streets and she didn't try to fight him; it felt so good to rest her head on his shoulder and let the rest of the world go by outside. 'You're exhausted, and you hardly ate a thing back there; we'll get something later at the hotel. Perhaps a meal in our suite—what do you think?' he asked tenderly. 'We needn't go down to dinner.'

She couldn't think about anything but how good it felt to be in the curve of his arm, pressed close to the big male body that had haunted her dreams for weeks. He was wearing a clean, sharp aftershave that smelt of lemon and musk and something else she couldn't quite place, and in spite of her panic and fear at what she had done there was a fresh riot in her stomach that had nothing to do with her damning secret and everything to do with Hudson.

'I don't mind,' she said unsteadily, keeping her face hidden against his shoulder. 'Whatever you want.'

'A beautiful *and* submissive wife,' he drawled mockingly above her head. 'My cup runneth over.'

Oh, Hudson, Hudson... Her conscience smote her again at the vibrant note in his voice he couldn't quite hide in spite of the light, teasing approach. However this worked out, he was going to be hurt, and badly. Suddenly the future wasn't so clear-cut, the web of half-truths and things left unsaid becoming even more tangled in her tired mind. She didn't know what to do any more and she was frightened, and so very, very weary of it all.

'Bill is sending a telegram to Keith to let him know how things are.' Hudson was attempting to defuse the electric tension inside the car. 'I've said you'll contact him yourself at some point to let him know if you're taking the job for Major Promotions or if you want him to cover it, okay? We can always have a delayed honeymoon if necessary; I don't want to interfere with your career in any way,' he added levelly. 'I want you to understand that.'

Honeymoon? *Honeymoon*... Deep waters washed over her head. 'Did you put my name forward?' she asked tremulously, moving out of the warmth and security of his embrace and immediately feeling bereft as the physical contact ceased. 'To Major Promotions?'

'Bill's family owns the company,' Hudson admitted, before adding quickly, 'But Bill did some investigation of his own before he went along with the idea. He's a businessman first and foremost, believe me. He thought you were a first-rate photographer, Keith too, so he knew he wouldn't lose out. The job begins this time next week so nothing's lost, Annie.'

She couldn't care less about the wonderful job, or her career, and even less about Bill Truscott losing out, she thought guiltily. The only thing she cared about was sitting right by the side of her, and she still found it hard to believe they were together.

Once they arrived at the hotel the VIP treatment was

out in full force, right down to roses and champagne in their suite. Marianne had never seen anything quite like the wedding suite, the bed easily eclipsing the one in Hassan's home in both size and splendour. It was sunk into the floor, the thick ivory-coloured carpet reaching down into its massive circle, and the huge, billowy duvet and scattered pillows and cushions reflecting the same varying shades of gold as the full-length curtains.

The rest of the suite was equally luxurious and unusual, the exotic mirrored bathroom having a small sauna room leading off its rear, and the sitting and dining area big enough to swallow Marianne's flat in London whole. There were bowls of fresh flowers everywhere, along with the latest books, magazines, baskets of fruit and all manner of chocolates and candies.

'Well?' Marianne was standing in the doorway to the bedroom, her stunned gaze riveted on the bed, as Hudson came up behind her after tipping the bellboy. 'Some pad, eh Mrs de Sance?'

'Don't…don't call me that.' It wasn't the most tactful thing she had ever said, and she followed it immediately with, 'I'm sorry, Hudson, but I can't take this in yet.' But not before she had seen the mask he normally wore to the world fall into place, covering the tenderness that had been there a moment before.

'Sure, take your time.' His voice was cold, uninterested. 'Why don't we take a shower? Individually, of course,' he added with cool sarcasm as he noticed the quick glance she flashed his way. 'And then go down for something to eat? You could eat something now, I take it?'

'Yes, I'll…I'll be quick,' she stammered nervously, the thought of a shower with Hudson still sending delicious chills down her spine.

Marianne cried in the shower; she couldn't help it, despite telling herself she had to be strong, in control. If Michael had never entered her mother's life she would be the happiest woman on the planet at this moment, she told herself wretchedly—married to the man she loved with all her heart and who—she knew—loved her.

As it was… She shut her eyes, but the scalding-hot tears continued to flow. She didn't know what to do, and that bed… Would he expect to consummate the marriage immediately? Her heart leapt and raced, her confusion increasing still more. There was nothing she wanted more, but would it make it harder for Hudson when she left, or easier? How did men view these things? She really didn't know. She sank down onto the floor of the shower, her misery swamping her along with the silky warm water.

She heard Hudson call her name, a concerned note in his voice that told her she had been in the shower far too long, and she tried to answer him but her tears strangled the words in her throat. And then he was there, in the bathroom, his outline visible through the heavy plastic cubicle. He had stripped in anticipation of his own shower and was naked but for the small towel draped about his hips; that much registered as he slid back the door of the cubicle with a force that spoke of his panic.

'What the hell…?' And then he had gathered her into his arms as the water continued to cascade over both of them, lifting her weight as easily as if she were a tiny child.

She continued to sob against the muscled warmth of his body, all her efforts to control the weeping useless, and he carried her over to the big basket chair in one corner of the room, sitting down with her on his lap and wrapping a huge fluffy bath towel around her shaking body as he held her against his chest.

'Enough, enough, my love; you are making yourself ill.' She heard him but she couldn't respond, the exhaustion and desolation of weeks, if not years, culminating in a release of emotion that was unstoppable, and she abandoned herself to the flow.

He continued to cradle her close, saying nothing more beyond soft, soothing sounds as he stroked the hair back from her forehead and hot cheeks. She cried until there were no more tears left and her misery had settled into the odd hiccuping sob as she lay spent and still in his arms.

'I have to say, in all my years of adulthood, I have never had a woman so distressed at the thought of sharing my bed.' His voice was gentle and deep, and it was meant to be playful, but she couldn't bear him thinking that and turned blindly into his chest, nuzzling her head against his throat as her arms went round his neck.

'Listen, Annie, listen.' His voice was husky but controlled. 'I don't know what's wrong, but I can wait, do you understand me? If this is anything physical, if you're frightened or you've been hurt in the past in some way, there's no need to do anything you don't want to do merely because of a ceremony and a few words spoken over us. I wanted to marry you because I want *you*; get that into your head. All of you—heart, soul and body—and if that means waiting until you're ready for the physical side of marriage I'll wait. There's nothing, absolutely nothing, to be scared of.'

Oh, if only he knew, she thought wretchedly. 'Hudson—'

'I mean it, Annie. Nothing can hurt you now; I won't let it.'

Marianne could feel his heart slamming against the solid wall of his chest like a sledge-hammer, the bunched muscles in his arms as he held her, while restraining her too, hard and strong.

'You don't understand.' She raised her head to look into his face, her eyes swollen and drowning pools of pain. 'It's all so complicated.' She shifted in his arms, her hands lifting to his shoulders again. 'But I do want you; I do, I do.'

'Annie...' His voice was a groan. 'I want to give you time, damn it, but, holding you like this, I can't think straight.' He made to put her away from him but she clung all the tighter.

'I don't want to talk.' She lifted her mouth to his. 'I
want *you*. I'm not frightened; I could never be frightened
of you.'

'Annie, this is no game. If I start to make love to you
now I shan't be able to stop; do you understand that?
Hell, I've waited so long—'

'I know, I know.' His tenderness, his effort at understanding while not understanding a thing had melted the
last of her resistance, and she was powerless against the
flood of love and desire that was carrying her along in
its path. She wanted him, she needed him, and whether
it was right or wrong this was their wedding night. 'I
want you, Hudson, so much. I love you so much…'

He stood up with her in his arms, the towels falling
from their bodies, and as she saw their reflection in the
mirrored walls she saw the huge arousal he had been
trying to control. He kissed her as he carried her back
into the bedroom, filling her with the thrusting taste of
his tongue as he crushed her softness against him and
biting her lips with tiny little nips that caused her to
moan and arch in his arms as she sought greater inti-
macy.

When he stepped down onto the bed and sank down
with her into the scented, billowy mass she opened her
eyes to meet his, the expression in the smoky grey
depths causing her to murmur his name lovingly.
'You're beautiful, so, so beautiful,' he whispered softly.
'Your first time should be gentle and slow, but I want
you so much…'

But then, as he stretched out beside her, the control
was back, his kisses tender and erotic as he touched and
tasted her with a delicate sensuality that roused her to
fever pitch. She couldn't believe what was happening to
her body, the way his lovemaking was making her feel,
so bewildered by the mounting pleasure his intimate, experienced assault was causing that time and reason stood
still.

He explored every inch of her, his mouth and hands

creating a dizzyingly hot desire that expressed itself in little whimpers of frustration, the core of her becoming meltingly moist and ripe. And still he resisted the urge to take her fully, bringing her to the brink of fulfilment time and time again only to draw back at the last moment as she moved restlessly, urgently against him.

Marianne was too inexperienced to appreciate the extent of the restraint his love had placed on him as he sought to put her pleasure before his; she only knew that if the world stopped at that moment—if the universe exploded in a million tiny pieces—it wouldn't matter. All that mattered was Hudson and what his hands and mouth were doing to her.

The dusky shadows of evening were darkening the room when he at last lifted her hips up to meet the hard power of his manhood, but even then he eased his way into the tight, warm, secret place with a finesse that made his swollen fullness easy to accept. He caught her brief gasp of pain with his lips, stilling instantly and allowing her body time to adjust to the alien presence inside it, and then he began to move slowly, smoothly, his body dark and muscled against her soft fairness.

She wouldn't have believed she could experience such rhythmic, explosive rapture and not die from it, and as she began to move herself, welcoming him further, deeper, the last of Hudson's control was burnt up in the peaks of pleasure they were both experiencing.

She wasn't aware of calling his name in the moment they both tipped over the pinnacle into a fiery world of colour and light and sensation, only of his fierce and savage cry of exultation as he made her wholly his and took her with him to the stars.

Marianne came back slowly from the warm, satisfying completeness of that other world, an exhaustion so deep as to be paralysing drugging her senses as she lay in the curve of Hudson's arm, snuggled up against his warm, hairy body with her face on his furry chest as he kissed the top of her head and held her close.

She must have slept, because when she next opened her eyes it was to a room filled with the half-light of dawn, and she was still encircled by Hudson's body, safe and secure and content. She couldn't remember sleeping like that for years... The thought was there, in the soft golden moment before she became fully awake, but then her eyes shot open as she remembered. *Hudson*.

She froze before moving carefully, experimentally, easing herself out of his protective embrace and sliding slowly towards the edge of the bed. What had she done? *What had she done?*

She shouldn't have slept with him, not so...so completely, she told herself desperately. She should have let it be a physical mating, a fleshly thing. She shouldn't have given herself to him heart, soul and body, because he'd know—he would have sensed—her utter abandonment, and it would make their subsequent parting so much more difficult for him to accept. Little chills of sick panic flickered up and down her spine. But how could she leave him now?

'Where do you think you're going?'

Hudson's voice was soft and satisfied, and Marianne froze again at the edge of the vast bed before turning slowly to face him, the edge of the duvet clutched against her breasts.

'I...I need to go to the bathroom,' she managed at last.

He raised himself into a leaning position on one elbow, his powerfully muscled chest causing her breath to catch in her throat as he drawled, 'Hurry back, sweetheart.'

'Sweetheart'. She continued to sit there staring at him, noticing the tender amusement in his handsome face as he studied her confusion. He thought she was shy, embarrassed at all the intimacies of the night before, she thought helplessly, and perhaps if the situation had been different she might have been. But there was no room for maidenly modesty now. She was going to have to tell him; she should have told him years ago, because then it would have been cut and dried without all the equivocations and half-truths that had led them to where they were now. She'd made such a mess of it.

'Annie?' The lazy amusement had died to be replaced with concern as he watched her face. 'What is it?'

'I can't...I can't stay here,' she blurted feverishly.

'Here? You mean in this hotel?' he asked intently. 'But you were staying here anyway; I don't see what's changed.'

'No, not the hotel; I don't mean that.' Marianne swallowed miserably. 'I mean...' She closed her eyes, a hopeless sense of dark inevitability making the need to shut out his face paramount. 'I mean here with you, as...as your wife.'

She had expected an immediate response, perhaps a movement of his body as he reached out for her, but when the silence remained absolute she forced herself to open her eyes after long moments.

Hudson was still watching her, and as her heart began to beat in wild, panic-stricken little jerks he said evenly, 'Before last night I might have allowed you to get away with that, but not now. You're mine, Annie, and I don't mean because of a marriage ceremony either. There is no power on this earth that will make me let go of you now. You wanted me every bit as much as I wanted you last night.'

'You said—you said if I wanted to leave—'

'But you don't, not in here.' He hit his fist against his magnificent chest. 'This is telling you something different maybe—' he touched his head lightly '—but in your heart and soul you are all mine because you want to be, because you gave yourself to me last night more sweetly than anyone has ever done before. And don't deny it, Annie. I'm not a fool so don't treat me like one.'

'I...I can't stay with you, Hudson,' Marianne said flatly.

'Oh, yes, you can, Annie.' He moved across the bed,

careless of his nakedness, to catch her wrists in his hands as he knelt to face her on the rumpled covers. 'And you're going to, because I have no intention of letting you go,' he warned grimly.

This was worse, a hundred times worse than she had ever visualised, but now all her options were gone and she knew it was only the truth that would do. And whatever he said, however he manipulated the words in that astute lawyer's brain of his, she would know from his face that he was secretly horrified at what he had inadvertently let himself in for. His career meant everything to him, she knew that, and however much he loved her, however much he cared, a tiny, hidden part of him would be relieved if she left.

'You'll understand when I tell you,' she said shakily.

'I said I don't need an explanation; we've gone beyond that—'

'*I have to tell you.*' She cut across his quiet voice with a shrillness that silenced him. 'I should have told you before, long before, and then perhaps yesterday wouldn't have happened.'

'I wouldn't bet on it,' he said darkly. 'I love you, Annie, and that involves more than a quick tumble in the hay or having the little woman ready with the slippers when I get home at night. I'm committed to you for better or worse; I have been since the first day I saw you. I don't care what you've done or haven't done; there is nothing, *nothing*, that you could say or do that would make me love you any the less. So if you still want to tell me, knowing that, so be it.'

'Don't. Please, please don't.' The tears were running down her cheeks, the sense of loss already unbearable. 'Just…just listen, *please*, Hudson—without saying anything.'

'I'll listen.' He settled back on the bed, folding her against the hard wall of his chest so she was sitting with her back against him, his arms round her waist. 'Tell me.'

The moment was here, time had run out, and she didn't know how to start. She stared blindly round the beautiful room, cool and shadowed in the early-morning light, her nerves stretched to breaking point. What would he think of her when he knew?

'You remember that night, when you asked me to marry you?' she said, trembling. 'And I said—'

'You said "Yes, please, my darling",' Hudson said quietly.

'But I wouldn't have said that if...if I'd known.' She shook her head, the vibration of his heart against her back telling her he was not as calm and controlled as he appeared. 'But I didn't.'

'Known what?' he asked expressionlessly. 'What didn't you know?'

'When I got back that night, after you'd asked me, Michael was waiting to talk to me,' she said in a low, tight voice. 'He...he told me things—things that meant—' She took a deep breath. 'He told me he was involved with people, criminals, and that if I married you they would force you to work for them, or ruin you if you said no. They'd...they'd use your relationship with me to involve you, discredit you. He was talking about the big case you took on to start with, but there would have been other things, I know it; they wouldn't have stopped at blackmailing you over just that. He...he was so pleased I'd met you; he said it was a gift from the lap of the gods.'

She could still see Michael's face as he'd said it, the evil satisfaction in his narrowed eyes.

'My mother didn't know—please believe that; she was totally innocent. But...but I knew I had to leave her, and...and that I had to break all links with you, with Michael too,' she said stumblingly. 'I...I wrote the letters, one to you and one to my mother, and one to him too, and then I left France. There was never any other man, not ever. Not before I met you and not after.'

She paused a moment. 'I didn't know about the car

crash until months later, but Michael dying wouldn't have made any difference really. The men he worked for still exist; they know my name and they certainly know yours. You can't...you can't afford to have any link with someone like me. It would ruin you.'

Hudson still hadn't moved or spoken, and now, as she ran out of words, she waited a few moments before twisting in his arms to look at him. 'Hudson? Do you understand what I've said?'

And then she saw his face.

It was alight with relief—fierce, vibrant, joyous relief. 'And that's it?' His voice was husky, shaken. 'That's all it is? He didn't attack you, hurt you physically? That's all it is?'

'*All?*' She stared at him aghast, thinking he hadn't taken in what she had said. 'Hudson, they could ruin you; didn't you hear me? You have to be whiter than white, and I'm not.'

'I heard you.' He stared at her for a moment before shouting out, '*I heard you, I heard you. Thank you, God. Thank you.*'

'Hudson.' He'd wake the whole hotel. 'Don't you realise what it could mean to your career, your name—?'

Her words were cut off as his mouth came down on hers, and he kissed her like he'd never done before— not even in the midst of the wonderment of their wedding night—until her senses were reeling and her breath gone.

'Do you know the horrors I've imagined?' he said hoarsely. 'The things that have kept me awake night after night since we met again? A hereditary disease, child abuse, rape, even AIDS—and a hundred and one variations on any of those themes. Some of the things I deal with in my work are past belief, and suddenly they could have all applied to you. It's sent me crazy...'

'But this is terrible, isn't it?' She felt as though she was in a strange kind of vacuum, where black was white and white was black and nothing made sense. 'Those people know my name, Hudson. They *know* Marianne McBride. Michael was involved up to the hilt with them, and if you marry me and the mud starts flying—'

'I have married you.' He bent his head and kissed her gently on the mouth. 'Boy, have I married you.'

His voice was sensual and thick, and as she caught a reflection of the night before in his eyes she blushed hotly, before saying, 'But as Marianne Harding, and if I get out of your life before they put all the facts together—'

'To hell with the facts.' He took her face in his hands, his eyes blazing down into hers with an intensity that took her breath clean away. 'Don't you know how much I love you?' he asked softly. 'How much you matter to me? I nearly went mad when you walked out on me two years ago, and in Morocco, when you left...' He shook his head slowly. 'I never want to feel like that again. It was like the end of the world, and the worst thing was I couldn't make any difference to what was happening.' His voice spoke of the intense frustration and blinding pain he'd suffered.

'I love you, Annie, and everything else, *everything else*, comes second to that. You're the only woman in the world for me, *my* woman. I want you as my wife, my best friend, my companion, the mother of my children. Hell!' He stared at her for a second, a spark of anger in his eyes. 'How could you weigh all that in the balance and think I would put my *career*—' the word carried a wealth of scorn '—first, for crying out loud? What made you think you could make that sort of decision for me anyway? Did you have so little faith in my love? Think I was so shallow?'

'No, no, it wasn't that.' How could she make him see? 'But if you fight them, if it comes to that, and you lose— your name, your position, everything—how will you feel then?' she asked painfully. 'They could ruin you, Hudson; you have to face that. And...and then you might begin to resent me. Oh—' she stopped him as he went to speak '—I know you wouldn't want to, wouldn't try to, but you might, and…and I don't think I could bear that. But it would be natural—'

'Annie, I don't know what sort of men you've been used to being around, but believe me, no one I have any time for would think that was natural. You're as innocent in all this as I am, and as your mother was,' he added softly. 'I've seen plenty of low-lifes like Michael in my time; they're like ugly growths, and they can attach themselves to good folk as well as the other kind. They use people in any way they can and at any time, and are without mercy or conscience. I've fought them all my adult life and I know their tricks.'

'That's what I mean,' she whispered desperately, tears threatening again. 'They've good reason to try to get back at you. They'd always be there, just outside the perimeter of our life, waiting—'

'The hell they would,' he countered grimly. 'Do you seriously think I would allow you to live like that? They've taken two years of our lives; they aren't having a day more. Trust me, Annie.'

She wanted to believe him, wanted to trust in his absolute assurance of his ability to take on Michael's cohorts and win, but by his own admission these men would use anything and anyone to win. 'Hudson, they're dangerous. You can't expect to keep a secret like me from them, not when they don't adhere to any rules of play—' she began urgently, only to stop as his finger reached out to stroke the words away, his touch unbelievably gentle.

'I shan't be playing,' he said intently. 'And you are not, and won't be, a secret. I'm more proud of you than anything else in my life and I have no intention of not broadcasting that to the world. We aren't going to hide away, Annie, not for scum like Michael. They've touched your life through no fault of your own but they won't ever do so again; I'll make sure of that.'

She stared at the glittering hardness of his narrowed

eyes as he spoke, a chill slithering down her backbone. 'You wouldn't... You wouldn't do anything silly, would you?' she asked fearfully. 'I know you know a lot of people on both sides of the law—'

'I'll keep *within* the law if that's what's worrying you.' He grinned suddenly and her Hudson was back, although the brief glimpse of the side he showed in the courtroom, to men like Michael, had been terrifying. 'And now you don't have to think any more about it. You're my wife—I'm your husband—let me do the worrying, okay? From now on we face this and everything else together.'

His wife. Marianne's throat was dry. *His wife.*

'Okay?' he pressured softly. 'We're one now, agreed?'

'Yes.' She smiled tremulously, a dawning hope that it was all really going to be all right rising up inside her. 'But—'

'No—no "but"'s,' he said levelly. 'Not one single damn "but" between us ever again. Promise?'

She nodded wordlessly, her heart too full for speech.

'And another thing,' he added, his voice deep and gritty and his eyes loving her. 'The next time you want to save me from ruin, please discuss it with me first. I'm a big boy and I can take most things, but I couldn't go through this again.'

'Neither could I.' She tried to smile, she *wanted* to smile, but to her surprise she found she was crying again, the tears streaming down her face as her mouth quivered like a child's.

He knew the time for words was over and drew her down into the covers with a hungry tenderness, his eyes silver-grey as they held hers and his mouth passionate as he kissed away the tears.

Within seconds they were both on fire, relief and wonder adding an intensity to their love that was all-consuming. He moved over her, his lips claiming hers fiercely as his hands moulded her soft fullness into the hard, male planes of his body.

'Annie, Annie...' he muttered thickly. 'I could kill them for keeping us apart so long. They'll pay for what they've done.'

Her arms wound round his neck, her body moving almost savagely as she kissed him back with a wildness that spoke of her hunger and, touchingly, her inexperience. His mouth was branding her with heat, and then he moved away slightly and traced her throat, the soft swell of her breasts, her stomach and beyond with tiny, nipping kisses until she trembled helplessly, mindless with pleasure as she gloried in his need of her.

She arched and moaned against him, shaken beyond measure by the enchantment of his lovemaking, and her blatant need and desire took Hudson to the limit of his control as he moved against her convulsively.

His possession was fierce and absolute and her surrender complete, her body moving with his as she invited a deeper and deeper joining of their bodies, their lives, their souls. And when the moment of release came they went together into a glorious, shimmering world of their own, transformed, renewed, until their oneness was beyond the stars, the universe...

And afterwards, as they lay together in the warmth of their soft cocoon, the shadows of night fleeing before the brightness of the coming day, they talked and shared and made plans for the future that was now theirs to reach out and take. A future that would enfold children—warm, soft, vulnerable, precious little beings and products of their love—into their lives and hearts.

'No more fears, Mrs de Sance?' Hudson cupped her face gently in his big hands, his narrowed eyes searching hers.

'No more fears.' And this time she could smile, her face glowing as she stroked her mouth against the hard, bristly side of his chin.

'We're going to be happy, my love, more happy than

you could ever imagine in your wildest dreams,' he promised softly. 'I won't allow anyone, or anything, to spoil one more minute—one second—of our lives together. Trust me, my Annie—the best is yet to come.'

you could ever imagine in your wildest dreams,' he
promised softly. 'Hudson's silent support, or something, to
spoil our more intimate – our second – or our lives together, trust me, my darling, the best is yet to come!'

EPILOGUE

'THE best is yet to come'...

Marianne breathed in the warm, heady scent of a host of velvet-petalled roses as she reflected how often, in the last few years, she had acknowledged the truth of Hudson's promise to her that crystal-bright morning so long ago.

And the best had been good, so good. Her eyes followed Hudson as he played with their sons in the pool, three miniature clones of their handsome father and all with Hudson's considerable will-power, which made for interesting days. She smiled to herself lazily. But she wouldn't have it any other way.

Perhaps this one would be a girl? She stroked her swollen stomach thoughtfully. She would like a daughter, and she knew Hudson would too, but like the three before it this one would be loved for the precious and individual human being it was; its sex wasn't really important. It would be part of her and Hudson, after all.

And she had so very nearly missed being his wife. Even now she sometimes found it difficult to believe she had been so stupid, but she had been. Thank goodness Hudson was the man he was.

He hadn't waited to find out if her family association with Michael Caxton would become known, but with typical Hudson de Sance authority had announced it himself, and amazingly, through his many links with people working to smash crime from the inside, had identified vital new connections in organised crime. The tables had been turned and the arrests had been many. Hudson had won.

But all that had been ten years ago and she rarely

thought about it now—life was too rich and full to dwell on the twists and turns of the past, and the present and the future too precious.

'You're looking very serene, my love. Pregnancy suits you.'

She hadn't been aware of Hudson leaving the pool but now, as he flung himself down beside her on a cushioned sun lounger, she smiled dreamily as she met the wicked grey eyes.

'The best is yet to come.' She repeated his words softly, her eyes stroking over his hard, tanned body that still had the power to thrill her with so much as a glance or touch. 'Do you remember when you said that?' she asked tenderly.

'Of course.' He left his lounger to crouch beside her, before gathering her up in his arms and kissing her passionately, his large hands stroking over the swollen fullness of her belly as he murmured, 'And the story's not told yet. We're going to grow old together, see our grandchildren and maybe even their children if God is good to us. I think this one will be a girl.'

'What?' She stared at him, surprised by the sudden change of conversation. 'What made you say that?'

'Just a feeling.' He smiled at her, his grey eyes with their thick short lashes crinkling at the corners.

'Well, your feelings are always right.' It was a slight bone of contention that his intuitiveness was never wrong, whereas she could still make howlers at times, and she wrinkled her nose at him. She didn't really mind at all. To be close to him, to see him, live with him, love him, was all she could ask for and more. She was content to be wherever he was, and it was a good feeling.

'Aren't they just?' he said with the arrogant satisfaction that was such an integral part of him, before chuckling with amusement as she took a swing at his midriff.

'I'm so lucky, Annie.' Suddenly the amusement was gone and her Hudson, the Hudson that only she ever saw, was there in front of her, needing the reassurance of her presence in his life in a way that made her love him more than she could say. 'All the rest—the house, the cars, the boat, even the children—I could do without as long as I have you. You're all that matters.'

'Talking of children…' She winced as the pain she had been experiencing periodically for the last hour came more strongly. 'I think your daughter has decided it's time to be born.'

'*What?*'

Considering he had been down this road three times before he still wasn't very good at it, she thought mildly as her ruthlessly cool and intelligent lawyer husband turned to jelly in front of her eyes, sheer panic catapulting him to his feet.

'But it's not time—you've still three weeks to go.' He eyed her, horror-stricken, and she couldn't prevent a giggle from escaping her lips despite the power of the contraction.

'Perhaps you'd better tell the baby that,' she said with the sereneness he'd spoken of earlier, protesting only slightly when he whisked her up in his arms, shouting to their au pair—a stout, solid girl whom the children adored—to look after the boys as he turned and made for the house.

By the time they got to the hospital a few blocks away from their sumptuous home in the suburbs of Washington DC, the contractions were coming hot and strong, and Marianne was too preoccupied with her breathing exercises to care about anything else.

She was aware of Hudson shouting orders at everyone within earshot, and then later, once they were established in a little room of their own with the requisite doctor and nurse, of her unflappable husband flapping frantically, but all her energy and resources were concentrated on the new life inside her struggling to be born.

It was two hours later before their perfect little daughter was born, pushing her way into the world with a determination that was all Hudson, but looking amazingly like her beautiful mother. She was a small baby, but with a feminine delicacy rather than frailness, and had a shock of blonde hair that was positively luxuriant. She didn't resemble her three dark little brothers at all.

Marianne let her head fall back against the pillows as Hudson took their daughter from the nurse and placed her in Marianne's arms.

'She's beautiful.' He had been moved at his sons' births, but this was the first time she had seen him cry. 'She is so beautiful, and she is the image of you,' he said with a shaky wonder that made Marianne's eyes misty too. 'Our daughter; we have a daughter. I…I can't believe it.'

'I thought you knew.' She smiled up at him through her tears of joy. 'You seemed very sure about her earlier if I remember.'

'But now she's here…' He couldn't take his eyes off the sweet little face cocooned in the hospital blanket. 'She's real.' His gaze moved to Marianne's tired but glowing face. 'I love you, Mrs de Sance,' he said softly, and she knew, without knowing how she knew, that he was remembering his mother and his own wretched childhood, and how different they had made things for their own family. Each one treasured and loved. Each one wanted.

'I love you, so much.' Her heart was in her eyes.

Later, when Jane Marianne was lying in her bassinet by the side of the bed, Hudson drew Marianne close to him, the tightness of his embrace echoed in her own heart.

He was her sun, moon and stars, as she was his, and together they had defeated all the ghosts from the past. Michael and his colleagues, Hudson's mother and father—they were just memories now, and they had lost the power to sting and hurt. Everything that had made up their lives before they had met was shadowy and unreal, she reflected silently as Hudson held her close.

She was cherished, adored, and she knew she could

face anything that might happen in the future with Hudson at her side. To wake up beside him in the morning, to feel his arms around her at night in the tender afterglow of lovemaking—it was all she could ask from life and more.

She reached for his lips now, twisting against him as her mouth sought his in a kiss that was as fierce and hungry as ever. He was all she had ever wanted—all she could want. Their life had begun when the wedding bells had stopped.

If you enjoyed what you just read,
then we've got an offer you can't resist!

Take 2 bestselling love stories FREE!

Plus get a FREE surprise gift!

Celebrate **15** years with

HARLEQUIN®

I N T R I G U E®
Because romance is the ultimate mystery...

*It's been 15 years since Harlequin Intrigue®
premiered—and we're still leaving you
breathless with pulse-pounding suspense
that heightens and electrifies romance to
keep you on the edge of your seat.*

Check your retail outlet for some of your favorite
Intrigue® authors and books!

✔ **43 LIGHT STREET** by Rebecca York
✔ **FEAR FAMILIAR** by Caroline Burnes
✔ **THE LANDRY BROTHERS**—a *new* series
from Kelsey Roberts
✔ **COUNTDOWN 2000**—a special millennium
promotion from three of your favorite authors!

Dynamic life-and-death stories with a
happy ending that you can find only at

HARLEQUIN®

I N T R I G U E®

HARLEQUIN®
Makes any time special ™

Coming Next Month

HARLEQUIN ⬥ PRESENTS®

THE BEST HAS JUST GOTTEN BETTER!

#2049 MISTRESS BY ARRANGEMENT Helen Bianchin
(Presents Passion)
Michelle is stunned when wealthy businessman
Nikos Alessandros asks her to be his social companion for a
few weeks. Will Michelle, under pressure from her family to
make a suitable marriage, find herself becoming a mistress
by arrangement?

#2050 HAVING LEO'S CHILD Emma Darcy
(Expecting!)
Leo insisted she marry him for the sake of their unborn child.
But despite his fiery kisses, Teri couldn't forget that Leo had
never considered marrying her before she got pregnant.
Could they turn great sex into eternal love?

#2051 TO BE A BRIDEGROOM Carole Mortimer
(Bachelor Brothers)
Jordan is the youngest Hunter brother. His devilish good
looks have helped him seduce any woman he's ever wanted—
except Stazy. There's only one way for Jordan to get to the
head of Stazy's queue—become a bridegroom!

#2052 A HUSBAND OF CONVENIENCE Jacqueline Baird
When an accident left Josie with amnesia, she assumed that
her gorgeous husband, Conan, was the father of her unborn
baby. They shared passionate nights until she remembered
that theirs was actually a marriage of convenience....

#2053 WEDDING-NIGHT BABY Kim Lawrence
Georgina decided she couldn't attend her ex-fiancé's wedding alone—she needed an escort! Callum Stewart was
perfect: gorgeous, dynamic...and on the night of the
wedding he became the father of her child!

#2054 THE IMPATIENT GROOM Sara Wood
(Society Weddings)
Prince Rozzano di Barsini whisked Sophia Charlton away to
Venice in his private jet. One whirlwind seduction later, she'd
agreed to be his bride. But why was Rozzano in such a hurry
to marry? Because he needed an heir...?